Are you ready to take that risk?

- Do you feel you deserve more recognition on the job, but aren't getting it?
- Do you go along with what your partner wants to do... and deny your own feelings?
- Do you avoid conflict and confrontations at all costs?
- Do you act as if your needs don't really matter?
- Do you feel stuck?
- Do you hate your job?
- Is there a problem at home you aren't dealing with?
- Do you dislike where you're living?
- Do you long for adventure?
- Are you bored?
- Are you different on the inside from what people see on the outside?

SUCCESSFUL RISK-TAKING CAN BE YOUR ROAD TO HAPPINESS AND FULFILLMENT. FIND OUT HOW WITH...

GO FOR IT!

BETSY MORSCHER is an international business consultant who has designed creative stress management programs for business, industry, and conventions. She lectures to thousands of people every year. The president of her own company, Personal Energy Programs, she is also an educator, lecturer, and author of *Heal Yourself the European Way*. She lives in Denver, Colorado.

BARBARA SCHINDLER JONES is a communications consultant, teacher, trainer, speaker, and president of Communication Resources. She is the author of more than one hundred articles, features, and short stories, and has been author or co-author of four books, including *Successful Negotiating Skills for Women*. She lives in Boulder, Colorado.

UPDATED EDITION

GO FOR IT!

SUCCESSFUL RISK-TAKING FOR WOMEN

Betsy MORSCHER

& Barbara SCHINDLER JONES

(formerly published in hardcover
under the title: *Risk Taking for Women.*)

WARNER BOOKS

A Time Warner Company

WARNER BOOKS EDITION

This Warner Books edition is published by arrangement with the authors.

Cover design by Susan Newman

Warner Books, Inc.
1271 Avenue of the Americas
New York, N.Y. 10020

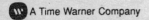 A Time Warner Company

Printed in the United States of America

First Warner Books Printing: May, 1992

10 9 8 7 6 5 4 3 2

DEDICATION

To Amy Goodhue Loomis, an inspiring teacher who
encouraged me to risk being my best; and

To Sean Yancey, a visionary whose entrepreneureal spirit
encourages me and a myriad of other women to go for it.

BETSY

To my father, F.C. "Mike" Schindler, who was a consummate
risk-taker and influential role model; and

To Professor Thorrel B. Fest, who gave me a leg up on the
risking ladder and still stands by to break my fall.

BARB

Life is either an incredible adventure or it is nothing.

HELEN KELLER

CONTENTS

PREFACE

SAFETY and security are important human values. From our first safe and secure place, the womb, we are thrust into life, the most risky proposition of all. Do we have a subconscious wish to return to the womb? Is that why some people—particularly women—opt for warmth and being sheltered above all?

Choosing the security option is okay if that is the way to achieve what you want most out of life. But we decided to write this book for those women who wondered, "Is that all there is?" and for those who now question if being safe and warm is all that wonderful. We felt this book could help women who want to go for the gusto and become more self-fulfilled and self-actualized.

Risk-taking is somehow associated with being American. Think of the early explorers, trappers, and all those pioneers bouncing to the West in their covered wagons. In modern times, think of the builders, the scientists, and the breathtaking risk of flying to the moon.

Women were right there risking with their fathers, husbands, and brothers in earlier times. They even won the vote. Then something happened. Was it the depression of the twenties and thirties that made women lose ground? World War II brought more women into the work force, but after the war Rosie the Riveter was urged to "go back home so a returning veteran can have your job." Today, of course, women are entering and returning to jobs outside the home in increasing numbers. Some of them forfeit or postpone having families; others feel they can have—and manage—it all.

Many women have found themselves caught between their desire to be taken care of (because that's what they were taught to want) and their yearning to be free and independent. Being free also means taking on responsibility and being willing to take risks. Women have been held back from risking by conditioning, fear, lack of knowledge, inertia, and other barriers. Even those women who are ready and willing to be risk-takers find that they are unprepared.

Transcending corporate game plans, military strategies, and one-upmanship is one of our objectives. Another is to help women gear up for the twenty-first century by becoming the best they can be. Women can learn to recognize and use their own power, discover what they want from life, see it in their mind's eye, and go for it.

Although this book is directed toward the female faction, the information readily applies to males who also want to expand their risking horizons. We predict that one of the trends of the future will be men and women risking together, as creative and liberated partners, so that both are more successful at getting what they want. Therefore, this book is not intended to be another skirmish in the war of the sexes but to give women more tools in their long-playing game of "catch up."

Our ideas have been gathered from interviewing many women in all spheres, ages, and states along with examining our own lives and sharing what we've learned from mistakes as well as successes. Although most of the names have been changed for the sake of privacy, all examples cited in the book are true, not fictitious.

We ourselves have followed many risking paths, often against friendly advice from family and friends. After 12 family members died of cancer, Betsy risked mortgaging home and car to go to Europe to study preventive medicine. Her risks paid off. She discovered she didn't have to die in her 40's as had her relatives. She used this experience to write *Heal Yourself the European Way* and launch her career as a professional speaker and spa consultant. Barbara's risks have included a try at full-time freelance writing and starting her own consulting business with two women partners.

And perhaps our biggest risk was agreeing, on short acquaintance, to write this book! We risked merging our knowledge, experience, talents, and egos and have developed a process of working together despite different backgrounds and writing styles.

As you can tell already, we believe risking is worth the price. We believe the answer to "Is that all there is?" is NO! Whenever we feel stalemated, helpless, or hopeless, we know it's time to set some new goals and take a calculated risk. Whenever we admit that our lives are not what we want them to be, we know it's time to move beyond a safe, mundane existence and take a risk. Whenever we feel dissatisfied with career, marriage, relationships, friendships, or whatever, we know it's time to reassess, regroup, renew, and *risk*.

GO
FOR
IT!

ONE

RISKING MEANS TAKING A
CHANCE ON LIVING

COME on, Mary! Take a chance! Don't be chicken!" Did you hear taunts like that when you were growing up? Did you take the dare or did you hold back? If you took the dare, were you scolded later by your parents because *girls weren't supposed to take risks like boys?*

As you got older and went out into the world after an education, a job, a husband, a dream, what risks were you willing to take to get what you wanted? Like the turtle, did you stick your neck out to get ahead or did you pull back inside yourself?

Whether we like it or not, living and functioning involve risk. Getting out of bed, stepping into a bathtub, driving a car, being exposed to germs—these, and many other everyday activities we can scarcely avoid, involve risks of some sort. But to the co-authors of this book, the concept of risk means taking a chance on living—*really living* to the fullest. Risking means eagerly looking for chances to bring more joy, purpose, self-esteem, zest, accomplishment, and love into our lives.

In this opening chapter we are going to take a close look at what risk is and why so many of us work so hard to avoid it. We'll also discuss what it takes to be a successful risk-taker.

What Is Risk?

When you risk you allow yourself to be vulnerable to potential injury or loss. But when you take that chance, you are also opening yourself to the potential of reward. Risking means gambling, when you move from one place or situation or idea to another, that good things will happen, not bad. Risking means venturing out from the safe harbor to the open seas. In fact, the original meaning of risk from the Greek is: *to sail around a cliff*.

Risking is an invitation to be part of the action called life. It is clear that when you venture out into the unknown, where you cannot completely predict what will happen, you are taking a chance. Yet you cannot grow unless you risk. As long as you and your life grow and change, you need to find viable ways to respond. Risking helps you try on your options for size and decide how to improve the quality of your life.

What Kinds of Risks Are There?

Obviously, there are big risks and little risks; or you might classify them as high, moderate, and low. There are *personal* risks, where you take a chance on you and only you really know the internal risks and rewards you considered; and there are *interpersonal* risks, where you venture into or out of relationships and associations, or where you team up with other people for collective risking.

Most lives include risks that are *physical* (you might break your leg when you go skiing), *financial* (you might lose the money you invested) or *psychological* (you might get put down if you try to speak up for your rights). Notice all those "mights"; a very important word in risking.

Some people seem to thrive on the thrill of putting their lives in jeopardy; others are afraid to ride in an elevator. This brings us to an examination of *calculated* versus *hazardous* risks.

Hazardous risks are sometimes forced upon us—if we have to jump out of a window to escape from a burning building, for example. But many hazardous risks are taken voluntarily. Consider mountain climbing in a snowstorm, or betting your life savings at Las Vegas, or hang gliding in a high wind, or risking lung cancer by continuing to smoke.

An example of someone taking a hazardous risk was Penny, with few skills and the sole support of four children. She impulsively decided to give up her work as a receptionist in order to write her autobiography. Never thinking about how her actions would affect her or her children, she went on welfare while she tried to write. She became so preoccupied that her children were unattended and drifting around the neighborhood.

One evening her preschooler wandered down to a busy intersection and was almost killed. Still Penny continued trying to write. Finally when her children started begging for food, the neighbors reported her, with the unhappy ending that all four children were placed in foster homes. Penny never got beyond Chapter Two.

Calculated risks, on the other hand, are taken after you have done your homework, carefully thought through the pros and cons, considered the alternatives, and weighed the consequences of risking and not risking. Calculated risks require intensive planning of methods and strategies. You don't close your eyes and leap into a calculated risk. You know exactly what you're doing and what's at stake.

Although occasionally taking the plunge into risks that endanger your life, limb, or bankroll may be exhilarating, those are hazardous risks, which we do not discuss in this book. Nor are we including those few addictive personalities who become risking junkies. We are primarily discussing calculated risks from which the potential rewards are more tangible and worth going for. Going back to school, starting a business, applying for a promotion, getting to know yourself, taking up a new skill, venturing into a new emotional relationship, or trekking off to Zanzibar are all possibilities for successful calculated risk-taking.

What Happens When You Don't Risk?

When you see a chance to risk in order to go for something you really want and you back away from the opportunity, how do you feel afterward? You probably feel safe but vaguely uncomfortable. There may be a nagging disappointment in yourself, a loss of self-confidence, and your self-esteem may have slipped a notch. In a small but real way you feel diminished and less than you could be. In extreme cases, you might even succumb to illness.

Although Marsha knew that she had more qualifications than her present job required, she felt secure as a schedule coordinator for a transit company. When pinges of boredom crept up on her she became anxious. Should she try for a new position within the company? Would it be better to look for a job in another organization, or should she just be grateful she had a job? She brooded and stalled. The prospect of making a change and going from a secure known—even though it was, as she put it, "a drag position"—to the unknown, was frightening. She decided to stay on her present job and make the best of it. To deal with the boredom, she began to drink excessively. Four years after making that fateful decision Marsha knew it was wrong. Now her situation was compounded; not only did she still have to look for a new job, but she also had to deal with her drinking problem.

Risking exacts payment, to be sure, but the cost you pay for not risking is even higher. Without taking a risk, it is impossible to experience real love, acquire true power, or gain prestige. You cannot grow and become better than you are without taking a chance. Playing it safe is a luxury few can afford.

If you don't risk loving, you lose the capacity to love. If you don't think big, you lose the ability to think big. If you don't try the untried, the unknown becomes more and more frightening and is eventually avoided altogether.

That old saying, "Nothing ventured, nothing gained," makes the point that when you don't risk, you have no possibility of reward. But even if you risk and *fail*, you have gained something from the trying that avoidance of risk can never provide.

Why Are Many Women Reluctant to Risk?

Over the years, society (meaning both women and men) has dictated what the role of women is and how women are supposed to behave. The fact that different societies have promoted different male and female roles is proof that the roles are based on social rather than biological factors.

As the Women's Movement has made clear, there has been an emphasis on being ladylike and passive, to be chosen rather than to choose, to follow rather than to lead. Women have been expected to be the helper, the subordinate, the power *behind* the throne.

We now understand how important a part of our adult attitudes and values came from our playing with dolls and tea sets when we were young, while our little brothers were encouraged to build, to climb, to experiment, to kick, and to run. We read books in which Jane helplessly stood by for Dick to rescue her and in which adult women (our role models) were either sickly-sweet grandmothers or wicked witches.

Traditionally, women have been spectators to life's dramas; men have done the risking and women have cheered them on from the sidelines. Women have been conditioned to play it safe, and our success has been measured by the kind of man we were able "to catch" and how well we were taken care of.

Women are struggling to counteract their conditioning, but recent studies about how parents and teachers behave toward little boys and girls reveal that *the conditioning is still going on*. Parents often train their sons to be more strong-willed, hardworking, and ambitious than their daughters, who receive emphasis on obedience, good manners, and the expectation of being sheltered. Teachers usually expect boys to be more independent and take more responsibility, while their girl students are encouraged to be unselfish and nurturing.

In her book, *The Cinderella Complex*, Colette Dowling describes how easy it was for her to slip back into dependence on a man despite her years of successful independence. She feels women continue to want to be taken care of, to be relieved of the responsibility for themselves despite the long way we've come (maybe!).* Of course, each woman will have to make her own commitments and compromises but we feel any good relationship requires mutual dependence and we don't see dependence as all that bad, as long as it is freely chosen.

Many women have accepted the idea that they are second class, unprepared, weak, undeserving, and incapable of setting and reaching their own goals. It's no wonder that to them risking seems akin to falling off the ends of the earth! Yet when we look at our processed, homogenized lives that

*Colette Dowling, *The Cinderella Complex* (New York: Summit Books, 1981).

are a lot like white bread and refined sugar, we see that they
are not only bland but unhealthy. All the vital elements of
adventure and risk-taking have been persistently screened out
of them.

One significant factor is how women have learned to think
and feel about risking. To many women, risking has an all-or-
nothing aura, whereas men see risk as part of an ongoing
process that can be both positive and negative. Men look at
how a certain risk will affect their future; women are more
focused on the potential for immediate losses.

Fear is the big enemy. And considering our conditioning,
there are a lot of things that scare us—if we let them!
Women may fear *uncertainty* and the *unknown*. What is
lurking out there and what will happen to me? In a rapidly
changing world, we often feel we must hang on to whatever
solid turf seems to provide us even a small measure of security and order. We may hang on to an idea whose time has
passed, or to a dead-end job or an unsatisfactory marriage.

Another potential fear is of *disapproval* and *criticism*. Will
we still be liked and accepted if we break the mold of traditional roles and behavior? Many women who are now mid-
dle-aged, and attempting to take an important risk for the first
time, feel that their family's needs must continue to come
first. They have developed the notion that their job—their
reason for living—is to fulfill the needs of husband and children, while sublimating their own needs and values. One
such woman, who had spent many years doing charity work,
confided: "I am tired of being both hausfrau and chairperson
of endless committees. I want something substantial to give
my life meaning. If I die tomorrow, my tombstone will read,
'Here lies a superficial woman.'" Despite her strong feelings
of entrapment, she was afraid to risk her family's disapproval
by rocking their comfortable boat.

Another example was Arlene, a bright, attractive woman in the typing pool of a large corporation. She knew she had capabilities beyond typing and had been taking night-school courses to sharpen her skills in accounting, communication, and assertiveness. She hoped to move up to a more responsible job.

When a customer service position opened, Arlene wanted to apply but was fearful that she would lose the friendship of the other women in the typing pool. "It's as if we've taken a collective oath not to get ahead," she said.

But one night Arlene faced herself with the question, "Where are you going to be ten years from now if you don't try? Why are you holding yourself back?" The next morning she went to the personnel office and applied for the position. After three interviews, the job was hers.

But Arlene was still afraid to tell the other women in the typing pool. She managed to control her fears, however, and walked in, carrying a victory cake which she asked the women to share. Although some of the women were lukewarm about her promotion, others were genuinely pleased and said her pioneering efforts encouraged them to try, too.

Fear of *failure* is sensible when you are faced with wildly unfavorable odds. Taken to the extreme, however, you may allow this fear to prevent you from trying anything out of the ordinary—"Oh, I couldn't do *that!*"

Fear of failure, however, may really be covering up fear of success. We may have become so accustomed to not succeeding that success is as unknown as failure is familiar. Nothing recedes like success! But when success seems possible, it also is scary and may cause us to withdraw from the race.

We have all seen those few women at the top who have paid a high price for their success. They may exhibit a certain hardness or they may seem to be very lonely. Moving up may carry a price tag of broken friendships and the necessity of taking more and more, and bigger and bigger, risks. Women will become better risk-takers once they figure out that even if they do fail the world will not come to an end.

Our male counterparts have been exercising their options for centuries. Men develop and implement action plans for their careers as a matter of course and women are just beginning to acknowledge their own responsibility for lack of movement in their lives and careers. Women have not been encouraged to think in terms of career planning and implementation. True, they might have to get a job but they may think of it only as a stopgap until something better comes along. How many women even today think in terms of goals, both short-range and long-range, and map strategies for achieving those goals? How many women use a job interview as an opportunity to negotiate a higher salary, to ask about fringe benefits, incentives, and advancement opportunities?

Horizons for women are widening at last but thinking small is a hard habit to break. Women need to lift their eyes to higher aspirations and expectations. If you expect little, that's what you get.

Check the following adjectives that apply to you and your attitudes:

When I consider taking a big risk over something important, I feel

_____ scared

_____ exhilarated

_____ fine

_____ excited

_____ petrified

_____ challenged

_____ competent

_____ happy

_____ weird

_____ immobilized

_____ helpless

_____ nervous

_____ high   _____ confused

_____ unprepared   _____ confident

Fill in your own words to add to this list.

Now look at the words you have checked and added. What do they tell you about you and about your risk-taking attitudes?

The Process of Risking

Like a person forced to inch her way across a precipice on a narrow, makeshift bridge, you face the prospect of undertaking a risk. But before you decide to take that first step you need to know what is involved.

1. *Recognize the need to risk.* If you are not getting as far as you should in your career, if you are in a love relationship in which both partners are pretending that everything is fine, if you feel that you are stalemated and need to grow—if any of these conditions exist, then it's time to *do something*.

To risk means to act. If you want to reach your goal, you will have to forge ahead. The alternative is to rigidly entrench your fear and do nothing.

When you are considering a major risk, ask yourself these questions:

Is this risk the best way to get what I want or is there some other way?

What will I gain?

What will I have to pay or give up?

What facts, figures, general information do I need before taking this risk?

Do I have the necessary skills?
Have I made some unwarranted assumptions?
What would happen if I don't take this risk now?
Can I turn back?
What is the major goal I'm after?
How will I know when the time is right?
How much am I willing to bet that I'll succeed?

2. *Decide to risk.* Some people live lives of quiet desperation, on the periphery of existence. They are spectators of life's drama, dissatisfied with everything but apparently incapable of change. You know how hard it is to break a bad habit. Even if your life is like Mr. Roberts' ship, sailing between tedium and apathy, it isn't easy to admit that everything is far from copacetic and then do something about it. But psychologist William James summed it up when he said, "It is only by risking our persons from one hour to another that we live at all."

3. *Plan.* Make a plan for risking and then follow it. Have alternative courses of action in case of difficulty. Knowing you have viable options can often create impetus to work toward your risking goal.

4. *Follow through.* Make a personal commitment to risk. This is the moment when you declare your intentions and put yourself in the limelight. Committing to action invites other people to view your ideal and to watch you pursue it. Honesty in evaluating your risking preparations is crucial.

We'll have more to say about the risking process in later chapters.

Rules of Risking

Here are some suggested rules for risking which successful riskers play by:

Dos:

1. Have a clear goal and specific purpose in mind.

2. Consider your options and choose the most viable ones. Remember that risking opens up additional opportunities for more and bigger risks.

3. Get advice from people who have no stake in the outcome except for caring about what happens to you. (Before choosing advice-givers, however, take into consideration their own track records on successful risking.)

4. Always have alternatives as backup. The more options you have, the more leverage you can use. Another job offer, another means of income, new areas for developing emotional supports are all like extra money in the bank.

5. Be sure to take yourself into account. Do you have the abilities, the courage, and the knowledge to succeed? You as the risk-taker influence the risk and the outcome. There is a difference between taking a chance where you have no control over the odds and risking in a situation where you are a factor with some weight.

6. Do be serious about risking. Playing around when the stakes are high can relieve tension, perhaps, but could also get you into trouble by making you careless. Fooling or kidding around might also give you a reputation for being insincere or flippant.

Don'ts:

1. Don't count on always being completely successful or having one risk solve all your problems. Realize that each day may bring a *dynamic* risk, where gain and loss are pitted against one another, or a *static* risk, where the opportunity may simply be to consolidate and protect present gains.

2. Never risk more than you can afford to lose. Plan ahead. In the heat of the moment of risk-taking, we are less able to decide rationally what we can afford to lose. As a part

of your planning, set your personal limits and stick by them. Don't be pushed beyond what you decided to do before the crunch. There will be another day, another hour, another year. Don't be panicked into under- or over-risking.

3. Don't take risks for someone else or allow someone to take them for you. Take your own risks.

4. Don't use other people as an excuse for inaction. "I can't afford to return to school because my son wouldn't be able to go to college or my husband couldn't get the new car he wants." These excuses are just another way of saying that you are afraid.

5. Don't risk a lot for a little. Only you can decide what "a lot" and "a little" mean to you. But the principle holds.

6. Don't risk just to avoid losing face. From childhood on we are challenged to take a dare. We don't want to be called a chicken or a coward. Sometimes we say that we will do something that later turns out to be riskier than the returns warrant. We're out there on that limb and all good sense tells us to grab hold of the main trunk and get out of there fast. But we've made a public commitment and are embarrassed to have to back down. Face-saving is no basis for either risking or not risking. Retreat, which will allow you to risk another day, is better than a paralyzing loss.

7. Don't discount your intuition or your feelings. Does it feel right? Is your head telling you to go one way and your heart the other? Chances are what your heart is telling you is right for you. Be sure to get in touch with your feelings before you risk.

Rewards of Risking

Your reward for risking may be tangible (more money in the bank) or intangible (a heightened sense of well-being). Only you can determine the extent of the reward and how important it is to you. People who risk and win find their lives richer in all ways.

A word of caution, however. Because life is seldom logical or fair, rewards for risking may not always match up with the size and scope of the risk itself. But that can work both ways. Even little risks can sometimes turn up huge rewards.

Summary

To be more complete women, we need to challenge ourselves more. We need to create our own lives, assembling the best parts and weaving them together into the most fulfilling lives we can. Our lives can take on new meaning when we expand our vistas to include more and better relationships, when we set and achieve new goals and finally begin to fully realize our potential.

Dynamic lives are full of risks. We can choose to risk and make our world one in which we can function honestly with feelings that are authentic and acknowledged. We can choose to be freely and truly self-actualized. We can learn to risk and grow and win.

TWO

LEARN TO KNOW YOURSELF AND

PREPARE FOR A CHANGE

SOCRATES warned that the unexamined life is not worth living. Honestly examining our lives and ourselves is a real risk in itself. Will you like what you find out? Are there some aspects that you would just as soon not know? Will shining a bright light on all your defects and limitations be more depressing than instructive?

Take heart. You are bound to find beauty as well as blemishes when you clean out your psychic closets. Vow to be honest with yourself and make your self-examination thorough and true and therefore as useful as possible.

Begin by asking yourself some searching questions. Write down the answers so you will have them for later reference.

Your Self-Concept

Who am I? Don't slide past that one; it's not as facetious as it sounds. Write down at least ten words or phrases to fill in the blank "I am _____." What you choose to put down out of all the possible things you might include add up to your self-concept, or your idea of yourself.

Some people see themselves in terms of their roles. "I am a saleswoman." "I am a mother." Others would think first of their physical appearance. "I am blond and blue-eyed." "I am five feet five." Some people see themselves in relation to their strengths. "I am hardworking." "I am sincere." Others will focus on their weaknesses, or the aspects of themselves that they are trying to improve. "I am inclined to procrastinate." "I am not assertive enough."

What about your list? Did it emphasize role or appearance or strengths or weaknesses? Or was it a combination?

Now go back over your list and start crossing out those items that are least important to you. Among your multiple facets, which are key? Keep crossing out until you are down to essentials, until what's left is what you wouldn't want to give up. Now we're getting to the real you—the core, the heart of what you think you are.

Next, put down those words and phrases that best describe what you are *not*. This list can be as revealing as the first because what you put down here can have an interesting flip side. For example, if you put down, "I am not lucky," it may mean that you are relying more on luck than on making things happen. When an actor was congratulated on being lucky enough to get more and better roles, he answered, "It's funny, isn't it? The harder I work the luckier I get!"

Look at your "not" list in total. Does it represent characteristics that you are proud to lack, such as "I am not lazy," or those qualities you secretly fear you *do* have? Remember, all negatives have a positive quality behind them.

Here are some more questions to ask yourself in your search for the real you:

What were the seven most significant events in my life so far?

Why was each one outstanding?

What did I do to achieve them or make them happen?

How did I implement the process?

Now it's time to do some self-assessment around your history of risk-taking.

What is the greatest risk I have ever taken?
What was my goal?
What did I stand to gain or lose?
What happened?
How did I feel afterward?
How did it affect my later risk-taking?

In your quest for self-understanding, make up your mind that you will take the following risks:

1. *Risk being introspective.* Take time to be alone. Only when you are by yourself can you sort out your thoughts and feelings and be honest with yourself.

As you turn inward, try to understand how you got to where you are and why you think and feel the way you do. Temper your self-criticism with the positive. "I may be somewhat unsure of myself right now, but I'm kind of cute and I'm fun to be with."

2. *Risk being honest about how you really feel.* Get in touch with your own private feelings. Are you experiencing any emotions right now? What are they? When was the last time you felt very angry? What happened? How did you handle it? Were you satisfied with the outcome? When was the last time you felt truly happy? What did it feel like?

Feelings and emotions are the source of your creativity and energy; preventing their expression limits your growth. Some people cannot express their feelings because they don't know they have them. They have blocked off their ability to be in touch with their own real emotions.

It took an affair with a warm, tender man for one woman to realize she and her husband had stopped expressing any emotion to one another. Their marriage had become cold and routine and neither knew, or apparently cared, what the other really felt. "I was numb and lifeless around my husband but sparkling and alive when I was with the other man," she said.

Although the affair ended sadly in a separation for the sake of the children, the woman felt blessed and enriched by the experience. By allowing herself to feel again and to be vulnerable to hurt, she was no longer cut off from her emotions. The rich and deep feelings she had experienced with her lover showed her what she had been missing and gave her a goal to work toward in her marriage. With both husband and wife agreeing to work harder to communicate and to share feelings as well as thoughts, with both being more able to reveal how they really felt and what they wanted from each other and from the marriage, the relationship improved and is no longer dull and routine.

Give yourself permission to feel. Recognize how you authentically feel and ignore how you're expected to feel. If you are not honest about your emotions, you may end up pursuing the wrong goal, or the right goal for the wrong reasons.

What if the feeling you identify is good old-fashioned guilt? Deep down, do you feel you're not entitled to success because you're a woman? Or feel unworthy for some other reason? Somewhere there must be a "Sayings of the Mothers" that reads, "Thou shalt not be free of guilt." So many women have a mistaken sense of duty which dictates that they must have no worth as a human being separate from their families. They truly fear that if they get ahead in some way it means someone else is diminished.

Joan of Arc, take heart. Martyrdom is still in vogue.

A totally duty-bound woman often resents the giving she wraps in thankless and endless tasks. Her pattern of self-sacrifice, fueled by guilt if she even so much as thinks about breaking out of her self-imposed prison, results in excessive loving and giving. This is the point at which feminine rage may try to emerge and, like the guilt, be submerged and repressed.

Before the rage is acknowledged, the first reaction is usually to deny. What? *Me* angry? Nonsense! If you are in this situation, you need to get the anger out and verbalized. Dare to say, "I am angry, damn it!" Admit that you do have feelings and are entitled to them. Repeat "I am angry, damn it!" at least three times, making each one louder than the one before. Pound a pillow and release all that built-up tension.

3. *Risk admitting you aren't perfect.* When you are able to admit that you have, at least occasionally, been wrong or made a mistake, you are free to move on and capitalize on your strengths and those many times when you were right. Admitting imperfections is basic to self-acceptance and also provides the groundwork necessary for growing and improving. After all, if you're perfect, you have no need for education and change. What's more, if you have gone through life without meeting failure, then you are probably playing it too safe and are not challenging yourself enough to grow.

4. *Risk letting go of outmoded attitudes and excuses.* Ask yourself if you are willing to give up superficial attachments, destructive habits, and false beliefs that impede your progress. Deliberately discard such ideas as "I am not entitled to success," or "I still have children at home so I can't risk going back to school." Look at the can'ts in your life and see if they aren't really won'ts, or somebody else's shouldn'ts.

One woman who allowed a destructive habit to hold her back was Gloria. After her divorce, suddenly finding herself with the full financial responsibility of raising two children, she took the first job available, as a bookkeeper in a department store. Self-pity and money worries caused Gloria to become fifty-plus pounds overweight. She used candy to reward herself, rationalizing that, after all, candy bars didn't cost much money and she needed something to soothe her frayed nerves.

When a co-worker would comment about her rapid weight gain, Gloria would respond, "I've always had a problem with my metabolism. Actually, I eat very little." The latter part was true; she did eat little, but what she ate was high in calories and continued to add to her ballooning figure. Gloria refused to admit to herself that her habit of overeating and consequent weight increase were not only affecting her health, but were also affecting her chances for new career directions, which she secretly wanted.

One evening while attending a back-to-school night at her children's school, Gloria ran into a former friend who didn't even recognize her. At last, Gloria took a long overdue and honest look at herself and vowed to take action.

After five months on a weight-loss program, Gloria has a new image, a new job, and a new approach to life. She freely admits that it would not have happened if she had not faced and given up her bad eating habits.

Is an outmoded attitude or bad habit holding you back? Fear and inertia hold many women tightly in an uncomfortable place, while others elect not to give up the closet drinking or use of drugs that serve as their crutches. Destructive habits can only put people in double binds. Which risk is greater? Giving up the habit and risking moving into the world and taking your chances, or continuing the habit and putting a high risk on your health?

5. *Risk being you and only you.* The purpose of your self-assessment is to identify the unique person you are—the original you, not a carbon copy of someone else. No other risk seems so fearful as consciously dropping all the masks and façades and simply being you. Yet no other risk is so easy to maintain once it has been experienced and becomes a habit. Being yourself is actually a lot easier than playing a role, or

acting in certain ways because you believe that is what is expected of you.

Risk being yourself and get beyond appearances and what other people may think. If you realize you are keeping a tight control on your feelings in order to protect someone else, ease up and become more authentic for the sake of your mental health. Suppressed anger can turn into depression, which serves neither you nor anyone else.

Your self-concept has taken a lifetime to develop. You learned which of your actions pleased or annoyed your family, teachers, and friends. You learned how to see yourself from the way others saw you and reacted to you. Your idea of who you are has been shaped by your learning which attitudes, beliefs, and behaviors to keep and which to discard. Who you *think* you are is more important than who you *really* are.

Perhaps right now you're thinking there is a danger in too much introspection, that it's time to get beyond the self-centeredness or what has been called the "Me Decade." We agree with that because we are not advocating self-centeredness or selfishness; we are trying to convince you that any attempt to grow and change must begin with self-assessment and self-understanding. There can never be too much self-analysis because the search for self is as unlimited as our exploration and understanding of the cosmos. We don't even know how many galaxies and planets there are out there. Similarly, none of us truly knows how many facets there are within us.

Actually, there is no more rewarding search for women today than the search for selfhood. Today it's okay to be a person in your own right, a whole person and not a half of someone else. By first turning inward, women today can look more clearly outward and onward.

One Woman's Struggle for Self-Identity

Anne had played the maternal and wifely role of vicariously living and achieving through her family. She wanted to be an entity in her own right. After the family went to bed each night, she would pace the floor, chain-smoking. "What can I do with my life? I am forty years old and my life is probably more than half over. Where do I go from here?" she'd ask herself, but there didn't seem to be any answer.

She listed things she was good at. She looked in the Yellow Pages for possible vocational ideas. Secretary? Nurse? Out! Other traditional women's roles did not appeal either.

She paced and grew more anxious as time went by. Finally, close to a crisis level, she decided that since she seemed on the verge of death anyway, she would try writing her own obituary. She wrote about all the things she had done with her life that she could be proud to have appear in the paper. Then she began an even longer list of all those things she really wanted to accomplish, including earning public acknowledgment for achievement and for helping others to enrich their lives.

By dawn, Anne had decided upon her course of action. She would return to school and study guidance and counseling. That was ten years ago. Today she has a successful business of career planning and job placement for women. She is a sought-after speaker and travels widely to give seminars and help other women. The initial inventory of her skills, coupled with the writing of her obituary notice, gave her insight about who she was and, more important, who she wanted to be.

Exercises for Self-Understanding. 1. Take twenty minutes and list everything in life you would like to accomplish, every goal you have regarding your physical self, your relation-

ships, your work, travel, skills to develop, possessions to acquire, and anything else you can think of. Go back over your
list and indicate the priorities by marking the items A, B, and
C according to which you would most enjoy doing or having.
Then determine which you think would be most beneficial to
your life. Now you have an idea as to where to put your
energy and what you are actually most interested in accomplishing in your life.

2. Write a letter to your best friend from high school
whom you haven't seen in years. Tell her/him everything
you have done, seen, and experienced in the past ten years.
Be sure to list your accomplishments, your relationships, the
kinds of friends you have, your family, and anything else you
would like to say.

3. Pretend you have just inherited enough money to totally
support yourself for one year. You are entirely free and financially able to do anything you want for a whole year. The
inheritance specifies that the money must be spent by the
end of the year. What will you do for that year? How many
changes will you make in your life or your lifestyle?

Every risk involves some loss. Something has to be given
up in order to move ahead. Yet many women are terrified of
any possible loss and try to avoid all risks at any cost. In a
former era, they married and settled into relationships that
seemed secure. They seldom made waves at home or in organizations or church activities because they wanted to belong.
They often took and stayed with inane jobs because they
seemed stable. They were taught to remain on the sidelines,
waiting to be asked, never to initiate anything important
themselves.

The truth is that until women take the risk of unmasking
themselves, using the cold cream of truth and washing away
the subterfuge of fear, they will never find a sense of personal
acceptance.

Your Self-Esteem

After you have isolated your self-concept, or your idea of who you are, turn next to the esteem in which you hold yourself. If you have a positive self-concept, chances are good you also have a feeling of high self-esteem because the two are definitely related and interactive.

Esteem has to do with feelings of respect and worthiness. Here are some questions to ask yourself in order to identify the level of your own self-esteem.

Using a seven-point scale, pick a number for each question, with number 1 representing "No, never," 4 being "sometimes," and 7 standing for "Yes, always."

1. Do I feel sure of myself in most situations?

1   2   3   4   5   6   7

2. Do I feel that most people genuinely like and understand me?

1   2   3   4   5   6   7

3. Do I feel worthy of other people's respect for me?

1   2   3   4   5   6   7

4. Do I feel that I am fun to be with?

1   2   3   4   5   6   7

5. Do I feel significant and successful most of the time?

1   2   3   4   5   6   7

If your self-esteem rating scale shows a consistent lack of self-confidence and self-satisfaction, you will need to get to work at once. People with low self-esteem do not feel worthy of success and are therefore not apt to risk, even in small ways. If you can begin a program of positive self-awareness and self-development, do it. If you need professional help and counseling in this area, get it.

Since almost everyone on earth is lovable and capable in some ways, people with low self-esteem do not need to change themselves so much as change how they feel about themselves. They have to rid themselves of negative images. They also need to identify the source of their poor self-concept that, for whatever reason, has made them feel not okay about themselves.

Of course, this can't be done with a magic wand. You won't be able to wake up one morning and announce that now you feel okay about yourself. But you *can* begin immediately to lift yourself out of the doldrums. Start in small ways to emphasize the positive and not the negative. Determine to be in charge of your own success and your own happiness. Spend a part of each evening reviewing the successes you've had during the day. Oh, yes, you did have some successes! Maybe you resisted that gooey dessert. Maybe you wrote that long overdue thank-you letter to a friend.

Think in terms of goals and progress, no matter how small. What is something you'd like to become better at? What would you like to accomplish within the next five years? Get started and your self-esteem will take a forward step.

Another suggestion is to turn your attention to the needs of others. Nothing is so self-enhancing as reaching out to help someone else. Once again, these may be small steps but they *are* steps. Give someone else positive support by smiling at them, really listening to them when they talk, or by telling them how you appreciate them for specific actions or words.

Present someone you like with a gift for no reason at all except that you like him or her.

Try some analysis of how far you've come. Make a list of qualities or characteristics that you used to have but have no longer. Here are two examples: "I used to be overweight, but now I'm not." "I used to be lonely but now I make more of an effort to be with other people."

Your Attitudes, Beliefs, and Values

Since you weren't born with attitudes, beliefs, opinions, or values, you have obviously acquired them through living, observing, discussing, and experiencing. You started out accepting the concepts your parents and teachers believed in and taught you and then you modified these to suit new information and significant happenings in your life. How you think and act and what lifestyle you have chosen all reflect your personal belief system.

Although attitudes, opinions, beliefs, and values overlap and it isn't really important to try to separate them, it is useful to know that *attitudes* are commitments to behave in certain ways, *beliefs* are convictions about relationships between things, *opinions* are judgments that fall short of absolute conviction, and *values* are enduring beliefs that arouse an emotional response for or against them.

Attitudes, opinions, and beliefs are easier to change than values, which are at your very core. You have a set of values that are uniquely yours. You may have thousands of attitudes, but you probably have only a few dozen values.

Where and how did you grow up? Who were your principal role models? What is your earliest recollection? Does it illustrate any values that you still have or have since changed?

In our workshops, we find women who have difficulty answering the who am I question. Many have never thought about it.

If you found the question hard to answer, consider this: In his audiotaped program, *The Awakened Life*, Wayne Dyer describes a final philosophy exam he had to take in his doctoral program. Although the students had over three hours to write, the exam consisted of only one question, Who Are You? The hitch was that the professor told the class that none of the following aspects could be included: age, family, size, shape, color, money, goals, hobbies, religion, etc. What the professor wanted was a detailed description of the invisible part of the students without the use of labels.

Important values to you may have been more influenced by what you grew up without than by what you had. For example, if in your early years your family moved a lot, you may now place a high value on putting down thick roots. If your family home never changed, you may now feel the urge to travel and relocate more than most.

People are often unaware of their own basic values until they clash with someone who has an opposite value. Many women, when they try to identify and clarify their values, discover that some are more important than others to them. They may also discover that they have been living their lives according to someone else's values rather than their own. If you value home life and providing for a family, that's fine. But if you are staying home and doing homemaker chores not because you really want to but because society says you should, then you are not being true to your values.

If your life seems out of whack in some way, it just might be that what you say you believe doesn't jibe with how you behave. Books, workshops, and quizzes that clarify values can help people sort out what they really believe and help them program their lives accordingly.

Risk-takers usually believe that the world is an exciting place and who knows what's around the next twist in the road? They place high value on courage and adventure and like to live by as well as talk about their convictions.

What do you value most? Some ways to clarify your values would be to think about where you spend your time, energy, and money. A quick trip through your checkbook will tell you a lot. What, or who, now in your life would you most hate to have to give up?

Go over the following list of potential values and check those that apply to you.

Freedom to live your life as you want.
Accomplishing something worthwhile.
A long, healthy life.
Being known as a real and honest person.
A life with meaning and fulfillment.
Owning something of great value.
A chance to help the sick, elderly, or disadvantaged.
A secure and positive family life.
A meaningful relationship with God.
A beautiful home in your favorite setting.
Membership in a great health club.
A world at peace.
Being famous.
Salvation or eternal life.

Equality, sisterhood, equal opportunity for all.
A complete library of great books plus all the other books you'd like to read and own.
True friendship.
A college education for yourself and all your children.
Self-respect and self-esteem.
Opportunity to gain more knowledge in any field of your choice.

A physical appearance to be proud of.

Self-actualization, living and working to your full capacity.

A financially comfortable life.

Opportunity for unlimited leisure.

Time to spend with the religious figure you most admire, past or present.

A chance to rid the world of prejudice.

A perfect love affair.

Being popular and sought after by friends and acquaintances.

Success and satisfaction in your chosen career.

Unlimited opportunity to attend plays, concerts, operas, or the ballet.

For those items you checked, mark the most important ones A, the next most important B, and so on. It's okay to have more than one A or B or C. Don't worry about what it would cost or what others would think. Once you've got your clusters of most important values, study them and decide what they mean to you. Also ask yourself how they affect your life.

Now review the whole list of values and add any you think should be included. Rate them on your A, B, C scale. Last, cross out those that do not relate to you at all.

Congratulations. You have at least begun the crucial process of clarifying and understanding your values.

Where Do Your Dreams Go and How Can You Get Them Back?

It's a fairly well-known fact that human beings use only a small portion of their mental capacities. The brain requires exercise in order to develop, yet we solve many of our problems by habitual practices and comfortable routines that do not develop our unused creative capabilities.

Less well known is the fact that the process of tapping these reservoirs of latent possibilities is quite simple.

First you need to learn to trust your own subconscious and unconscious mind and then get in the habit of recording and remembering messages that surface. Analysis of these messages will soon provide patterns of information to help you understand yourself and to solve any problems that are nagging at you. Moreover, you can learn to deliberately program your subconscious so that you are guided to new insights and information.

The three major areas we are talking about and which many successful people have made work for them are:

1. Dreams
2. Visualizations
3. Affirmations

Let's look at each of these in more depth.

Dream Power. Dreams have a way of revealing missing links in our waking life, of pointing out problem areas which we have been trying to ignore or which we do not see clearly. Even dream fragments that we cannot recall specifically represent one way the mind has of trying to tell us something important. When we ignore dream signals, they recur and may even turn into nightmares if we refuse to get the message or act on it.

Throughout history people have regarded dreams reverently and sensed a meaningful relation between the inner world of dreams and the outer world of waking life. Hippocrates, the ancient Greek physician, practiced dream therapy. He also encouraged the ritual of dream incubation which involved a trip to a sacred temple, where one fell asleep in hopes of having a curative or prophetic dream.

One woman, who had suffered severe depression after the death of her husband, had a series of vivid red dreams involving her husband. The dreams helped her realize that her depression was the result of repressed anger at her husband for dying and leaving her alone. She shared her dreams and what they seemed to mean with friends to whom she could confide her feelings, and little by little, the dreams took on a white or healing color. Eventually she was able, in a dream, to say a final, forgiving goodbye to her husband.

Some people have found that fasting makes their dreams more vivid and easier to recall in detail. One such person was Bettina, a compulsive eater. Her marketing job for a large corporation was extremely stressful. Whenever she felt she could not cope with a situation, she would reach into her desk drawer and pull out some type of candy or pastry to nibble on until she got through the momentary crisis. The more job pressure, the more she ate. Finally, she decided to try fasting.

The third night of her fast, she had a vivid dream in which she was sitting at her desk being strangled by a marketing report and candy wrappers. Later dreams centered on her being in a small room that was filled with marketing reports and food piled to the ceiling. She was backed in a corner and could not move. She awakened from her dream perspiring and anxious. Only after she quit her job and went to work in a less stressful public relations position did the dreams stop and, at the same time, she was able to control her eating.

Several good books are available that can help you understand and interpret your dreams. But we believe the best book is the one that you write yourself. We advocate keeping a journal or a dream diary. Here's how to make this process work for you.

1. Before you go to sleep, place a notebook and pen beside your bed and tell yourself that you are going to remember your dreams and write them down promptly whenever you wake, whether it's 2:00 A.M. or your usual waking time. Re-

cord your dreams, no matter how fragmentary or unimportant or fearful they appear to be.

2. As you begin writing down your dreams, get an overall impression first. Take note of the setting, the people, the colors, the mood. Then fill in the details such as sizes of objects, facial expressions, time of day.

3. Realize no dream is nonsense. You are looking for insight and patterns, so don't worry if the dreams seem to make no sense.

4. Pay attention to the emotions revealed in the dreams. Do you feel fear or frustration or anger when you run down that dark alley?

5. Note your feelings upon awakening. Is it a relief to wake up or do you regret having to leave the dream? If the dream has great psychic impact, you may be perspiring and your heart pounding.

6. Pay particular attention to nightmares which are urgency signals that your inner self is trying to tell your outer self to take action about someone or something. Analyze all aspects of the nightmare for information and share the details with a trusted friend in order to reduce anxiety.

7. After you have kept the dream journal for a while, reread and review and look for patterns. Note the kinds of dreams you have in different locations, during different seasons or weather, or when you are with specific people.

Visualization Power. Anyone who has ever imagined being successful and creative in a given situation has used her visualization power. Advocates of this technique, however, are not talking about idle, pointless daydreaming but a specific process of visualizing what you want and seeing yourself getting it.

First, you relax and close your eyes. Next, you pay attention to your thoughts and images and deliberately arrange them as if you were directing a movie. Picture your goal and yourself enjoying your achievement. For example, if your goal is to lose weight, picture yourself as slim and energetic, surrounded by admiring friends.

People in all walks of life report visualization works. Athletes use it to mentally rehearse the perfect golf swing or forward pass. Actors visualize each action and line of dialogue in each scene. The power of visualization comes from consciously programming images of what you want.

The prospect of giving our right brain, which controls the imagination, a free reign may be alien to us. We are so accustomed to being logical and practical, we overlook the fact that the seemingly impractical imagination we have learned to disregard may ultimately be more practical, because it calls our attention to useful data stored in the subconscious.

Many successful riskers are very adept at visualizing their successful risks and goals in their mind's eye. In addition, they see themselves having some of the traits necessary for risking. Courage, tenacity, creativity, perseverance, and self-knowledge were described by successful riskers as some of the characteristics they saw themselves possessing.

One woman who was very fearful about risking used to imagine herself as a lion tamer in the circus. That occupation seemed courageous to her. Daily, she would forfeit a coffee break and go to the rest room and sit for a few moments and visualize herself cracking a whip and having three mammoth lions prance about at her direction. When she was finally ready to ask her boss for a raise, she spent her lunch hour visualizing herself first as a lion tamer, then walking out of the cage to the applause of the crowds and immediately into her boss's office where she visualized herself successfully negotiating not only a raise but a new position.

As the clock struck two, our would-be lion tamer walked into the corporate office of a major oil company. She took a deep breath and proceeded to state her case. Much to her astonishment, thirty-five minutes later she walked out not only with a raise, but with a far better position than she had visualized.

Part of your visualization should focus on how you would handle a variety of risking situations. Picture yourself dealing effectively with everyone. Even if none of the projected strategies is actually used, you have profited from rehearsing and will be less apt to be thrown by the unexpected. Worry brings negative images; mental practice gives you a positive ideal to strive for.

Here are some of the things you can do with imagery:

See your goal clearly and visualize yourself completing the risk to attain that goal.

Prepare for risking by stretching your imagination.

Find new ways to solve old problems and make decisions.

Become healthier and develop more viable health habits.

Increase your ability to learn to take chances.

Improve your skills for living and risking.

Expand your creative talents to risk and reach your goal.

Heal yourself when you are not feeling up to par.

Get beyond restrictive thoughts and into the freedom of your intuition.

Sharpen your perceptions and awareness about problems related to risking.

Discover your own special abilities, strengths, and uniqueness.

Increase your feelings of love.

Feel great.

Remember, the visual image represents your expectancy of the outcome of your goal. By changing your visualization, you are beginning to change your expectancy. The reason for reinforcing the visualization is that mental pictures provide a focus around which all the mental, emotional, and physical energy can organize. The stronger the visualization, the better job it does of focusing your energy toward goal realization and good mental health.

What you visualize matters. Develop imagery that will establish a positive expectancy. Put energy into solution.

Try visualizations and then draw a picture of your imagery. Add details like textures, shapes, sizes. What does it smell like? How does it feel when you touch it? What kind of noise does it make?

Draw or cut pictures out of magazines of what you want to visualize. Write a dialogue with your visualization. See a friendly animal sitting beside you and carry on a conversation about your imagery.

Before we leave the important subject of visualization, we must make a clear distinction between visualizing and fantasizing. Visualization brings intention, commitment, and trust that you will reach your goal. This means you are prepared to take action and follow through on whatever opportunities present themselves in your visualizations.

Fantasizing, on the other hand, usually centers on unrealistic dreams ("If only someone would leave me a million dollars"). We don't put energy into making fantasies happen but dream about other people solving our problems. Only we are responsible and only we have the power to control our destiny.

Fantasies are great for shaping the imagination and testing out ideas, as children do. They may even give us some insights. But fantasies do not have the power to create new realities. *

* Three excellent books for those who want to know more are: Adelaide Bry, *Directing the Movies of Your Mind* (New York: Harper & Row, 1978); Mike Samuels and Nancy Samuels, *Seeing With the Mind's Eye* (New York: Random House, 1975); and Shakti Gawain, *Creative Visualization* (Mill Valley, Calif.: Whatever Publishing, 1978).

Affirmative Power. Writing down affirmations can be used along with or instead of visualizations. Affirmations are a way of feeding your mind positive thoughts in order to get what you want. When you get behind your own power and agree you deserve success, then commit that belief to paper.

Pick a statement that embodies your main goal and write it over and over, at least twenty times a day. Such a statement might be: "I, Helen, deserve to get that promotion I have applied for." The more you write, the more convinced you become that you do, indeed, deserve to realize your ambitions and your dreams. The mental set of positivism is the catalyst that gets you going to work toward your goal.

Paste that statement of your goal in your calendar, on your desk, on the refrigerator. Let it be a constant reminder of what you want and your determination to get there. What we think about expands. So think about positive goals and never let negative doubts into your consciousness.

Patricia Barela Rivera, director of Dept. of Local Affairs for the State of Colorado, says that "It's a new time for women as power brokers in their own right. Women are now drawing from their internal power and self esteem to exert their power and influence in the community and workplace. Women are surrounding themselves with strong men and women who offer mutual support to bolster their confidence."

Ways to Prepare for Risking

Now you know yourself better and have some tools to help you keep in touch with the inner you. Next, let's chart a course for getting ready to risk in general.

1. *Observe.* Watch how other people risk. When you see a successful move or a good idea in use, make note of it and

add it to your repertoire. Keep your eyes and ears open for any approach or strategy that you could use.

2. *Talk to successful riskers.* If you have a mentor or helpful friend or colleague, find out how she does it. Ask questions. If possible, watch her in action and talk about how she risked afterward. If there is no one in your life right now who could serve as your advisor, seek somebody out. Arrange to meet someone you admire, someone who has been your secret role model. Most people would be pleased to be sought out for advice and counsel. If he or she is not pleased, find someone else.

3. *Read.* Watch for newspaper and magazine articles about people who have successfully risked. Keep those that seem most relevant to your situation. You might begin a risking scrapbook. Find books that will instruct, inspire, or motivate you to risk.

Here are some books we think you'll find useful: Marilyn French, *Beyond Power: Of Women, Men and Morals* (New York: Ballantine Books, 1985); Riki Robbins Jones, *The Empowered Woman: How To Survive and Thrive in Our Male-Oriented Society* (Hollywood, FL: Fell Publishers, Inc., 1990); Marsha Sinetar, *Do What You Love, The Money Will Follow* (New York: Dell Publishing, 1987); Stephen R. Covey, *The Seven Habits of Highly Effective People* (New York: Simon & Schuster, 1989); and Marilyn Loden, *Feminine Leadership, Or How To Succeed in Business Without Being One of the Boys* (New York: Times Books, 1985).

Of course you realize these are only a few of the ever-increasing supply of helpful books, many of them especially for women. In addition to those listed, you'll find we have quoted from or referred to several others throughout our book. We obviously recommend them as well. And be sure to read *this* book in its entirety.

4. *Do your homework.* Learn all you can about the facts and details involved in your potential risking situation. If you are thinking of starting your own business, get on the mailing list of the Small Business Administration. Find out how much capital is required. Investigate all relevant factors, such as location, financial backing, public relations, and staffing. Haunt the library; become a research analyst. Learn everything you can beforehand so that when you risk you are as fully prepared as possible.

Go back to school or sign up for the night courses or weekend workshops you need. What's more, be brave and go ahead and risk taking more difficult courses such as economics and mathematics.

5. *Experiment.* Before you go into the big risk, try out some ideas and strategies in smaller ways where there is less at stake. Test the water before taking the plunge.

If you have been using one style or approach and it hasn't worked, try another one. Don't make the mistake of merely working harder at your old style. Experiment with a variety of ways; try them all on for size and effectiveness. "I wonder what would happen if . . ." is a good beginning.

6. *Practice.* Try out your risking both in actuality and mentally. Practice some baby steps before you stride ahead. If you are planning to go for a big promotion, try negotiating for a better office first. Keep track of how well you did. Vow never to make the same mistake twice.

If you have completed steps one through six of your preparation, you are now ready to learn by doing. There's a lot to be said for on-the-risk training.

7. *Get on with it!*

Why Grow?

If you are completely happy with your life, you may not feel the urge to grow and change. But if you were completely happy, you probably wouldn't be reading this book. Trying to hang on to the comfortable status quo is an all-too-human activity. Don't rock my boat, please, I manage far better when the waters are calm and placid. Yet common sense tells us there are no handles on ~~the~~ status quo with which to hang on. The only constant is change.

People really don't have a choice. They *must* grow, they *must* change. The only alternative is death—either the fast or slow variety. Change can seem scary but not if viewed as adding to rather than taking away. Living *means* changing and maturing and re-creating ourselves over and over.

So why not welcome growth? Why not use the self-assessment process and the admitting of shortcomings as the foundation upon which to build a new you?

A deterrent to both growth and risk-taking is to hold on to bad habits. Clinging to old, familiar patterns because they seem comfortable and secure is programming yourself to fail. Self-help books aimed at growth and development won't help at all unless there is a commitment to act as well as read. Until we admit the complete truth about ourselves and our needs, we can never fully evolve into the persons we were meant to be.

Picture yourself opening to the world in the way a flower gradually unfolds its petals. See yourself taking on new qualities and skills. Visualize yourself whole and competent, and above all, be alert to all the risking opportunities around you.

Summary

Finding yourself and committing yourself to being you and to enjoy being you may be difficult. But the process of self-discovery and the setting of new directions can be the most gratifying experience you've ever had. To live life fully, be real and joyful. The more you know about yourself and the clearer you are about your goals and direction, as well as your needs for improvement and growth, the more successful you can become as both a person and a risk-taker.

THREE

GETTING YOUR REAR

IN GEAR

SUCCESS in risking depends on your willingness to take action—almost any action—rather than overestimate the pitfalls and possibilities of failure. Of course, there must be balance between reflection and action.

Now you know what risking is and how you feel about it. You know yourself better and have begun to realize how you want to change and grow. You probably also have a target in mind that you have decided is worth risking for. What's next?

Start by understanding that your life is a gift. You have been entrusted with hours, days, weeks, months, and years to invest as you choose. Have you ever thought about what you would do if this were the last day of your life and it slowly passed before you? Would you look back with pride at the way you invested your time or would you regret that you had never really lived? This special present was given to you and only you. How are you going to use it more wisely?

Your next step is to assume the responsibility for writing your own script and doing what's best for you. You determine where you want to go and chart your course accordingly. Refuse to let that anonymous "they" direct your destiny.

59

Do You Have What It Takes?

Now it's time to go over the characteristics and skills you'll need to be a successful risk-taker and see how you stack up. Don't worry if you come up short in some areas; we'll also point the way to where and how you can get help.

We have developed two lists of attributes that most successful risk-takers have: (1) qualities and attitudes and (2) knowledge and skills. Since all these concepts are valuable, we are discussing them in alphabetical rather than priority order.

Essential Qualities and Attitudes

Confidence (don't leave home without it). An old proverb goes, "Confidence is the companion of success." If you are confident, you are halfway to your goal; if you lack confidence it will show and out the window go your credibility and chances for success. Confidence in general means you are optimistic and forward-looking. Confidence in self means you're sure of yourself and your abilities, you are willing to be forthright and bold.

Both overconfidence and underconfidence are unproductive extremes. Overconfident people risk by charging out on thin ice or sawing off the limb they have just climbed out on. Underconfident people are afraid to try.

If your lack of confidence comes from lack of experience, the only answer is to get out there and try, even in small ways, to learn what you need to know and to set about acquiring that knowledge or skill. If your shaky confidence is related to low self-esteem, go back to Chapter Two and take a refresher on what might be done about that.

The confident risk-taker says to herself, "This is worth risking for and I am prepared to go for it. And I expect to win." Confidence in risk-taking is built on a track record of past successes. The second big risk is so much easier than the first. Moreover, if you have a sound and realistic self-confidence, you will not be devastated by an occasional failure. Instead, you will spend your energy looking for lessons to learn and ways you could have done it better.

Courage. Not all risk-takers are lionhearted. They may well be afraid but they have learned to face up to their fears and figure out ways to deal with them. It's okay to admit you're fearful as long as you decide upon a courageous course of action anyway. "Whistle a happy tune and no one will suspect I'm afraid." So goes the song from *The King and I.* Courage is often simply *acting* unafraid. After you have successfully acted that role a few times, it becomes a real part of you and not acting at all.

Flexibility. Opportunities to risk come in many forms and occasionally in disguises. Successful risk-takers can quickly shift from Plan A to Plan B when the situation or circumstances change.

You will find your flexibility increasing if you have planned ahead and prepared yourself for as many eventualities as you can imagine. What will you do if this or that happens? If your proposal is blocked at that point, what would a good fallback position be? If the give-and-take of negotiation is a part of your plan, you have both options and flexibility.

Imagination. Einstein once said that imagination is more important than intelligence. Using your imagination can give you a vision of the future and help you find more creative solutions to your problems. Can you visualize the perfect solution that would close the gap between what you have and what you have to have? People with imagination and right-brain skills not only lead better lives but also longer ones. It's true. Studies done on elderly residents of nursing homes throughout the country showed that those with an opportunity to take art classes or to create things themselves were far more alert and active and lived longer than those without these opportunities.

Are you able to tap your own creativity and imagination? Doing so often requires courage to forge ahead despite criticism or ridicule. If you can develop a "So what?" attitude toward your critics and let your own intuition take over, you have a chance to make the most of your imagination.

How might you improve your use of your imagination? (Don't say you lack imagination; nobody lacks it. It may have just rusted or gathered cobwebs from lack of use.) The best way we know is to turn inward, meditate, and listen to your inner thoughts.

In Chapter Two we discussed visualization power, in which you mentally practice a risking process. But here we are talking more about a mixture of imagination and hard work. Using your imagination effectively means you must know what you want, refrain from judging yourself because you want it, and give yourself permission to do what you want. Creativity flows when you are the one to choose what you want to do.

Some of the ways to increase your imagination and creativity are:

1. Start keeping a journal. Read it regularly for clues on what might be missing from your life.

2. Try something new. Get yourself out of your routine in some way. Learn a new musical instrument. Volunteer some time at a hospital or nursing home.

3. Spend time with younger people. Children are naturally creative. Perhaps you could teach them something and in turn be taught.

4. Work on an artistic project for which you feel you have a flair. Good at sewing, knitting, painting, refinishing furniture? Use this skill you already have to expand your aware-

ness of what else is possible. Take an art or a music appreciation class. Sharpen your creativity by learning more about
colors, fabrics, perspective, harmony, language. Broaden as
many horizons as you can. Work at perceiving more of the
world around you; take your blinders off.

5. Meditate. Be alone with your thoughts. Pay attention to
those thoughts.

Motivation. Your motivation, or the reasons behind what
you do or don't do, is an important risk factor. Lukewarm
appetites do not stimulate meaningful risking. Are you motivated to get out there and try? Are you motivated by the excitement of the risk itself? Are you hungry for rewards? Are
you moved to action by the triumphant way you will feel
when you win or by the proud look you anticipate on the
faces of those you love? All of the above?

As we all know, we are motivated because we have needs
and wants. At the basic level, we have needs to keep alive
and functioning; if we have a steady paycheck, this need
doesn't nag at us. Needs that could well be nagging at us
right now, however, are: to have people close to us, who
accept us and make us feel we belong; to gain appreciation
and recognition; and to be self-actualized, or the best that we
can possibly be. These psychological needs are more complex
than the bodily needs and their satisfaction, for the most part,
depends on other people.

You may risk to satisfy one or more of your current needs.
Your motivation to act will be high if you see a direct connection between what you want and the risks involved in getting it.

If you work in an organization, you are aware that an
effective team can form only when the needs of the individuals are integrated with the needs of the group. When managers complain that workers are apathetic, they really mean
that the workers are not doing what the managers want and

that the workers are not motivated in the same way the managers are. Remember our earlier discussion of generational values?

Although all humans have the same needs, people differ in the level and intensity of their needs and, therefore, in the commitment to risk at any given time. You and your best friend may both want to be promoted to the next level in your respective organizations but you probably differ in the intensity of your motivation to do something about achieving your desire.

Here is a list of possible needs. Check those that apply to you.

I have a need to:
    go along with group decisions
    strive for perfection and excellence
    avoid unpleasant jobs
    help others
    be alone
    have others do things my way
    get away from it all
    follow the suggestions of others
    avoid arguing or conflict
    have both long-range and short-range goals
    be different
    have affection from others
    keep busy
    be the center of attention
    try to do things better than others
    put things off
    be entertained during spare time
    follow habit and tradition
    keep from getting involved
    work no more than I have to

Add to the list any needs you have that are not included here. Next, rank the whole list according to how important each need is to you right now. Do you see some motivational pattern emerging?

Present and future orientation (not past). Your daydreaming and wishful thinking are clues to what you consider your possible dream and whether you are past-, present-, or future-oriented. Do you daydream about "I wonder what would have happened if. . . ?" "I wonder what would have happened if I had taken that job instead of this one, had married Bill instead of Bob, had kept up my piano lessons. . . ?" Successful people learn from the past but don't live in it. Their visions take the form of what is apt to happen if they do A or B or C. Their focus is on being alert to future, not missed, opportunities.

Self-discipline. Are you hard or easy on yourself or somewhere in between? For instance, do you climb quickly out of bed even though you'd rather go back to sleep? Do you pass up a delectable dessert to stay on your weight-loss program? Do you turn down social invitations in order to achieve goals and meet deadlines?

If you answered all these questions with a "Yes, always," you're probably too hard on yourself and are setting yourself up for some future blowup of oversleeping, food binges, or missed deadlines. If you answered, "Yes, mostly," your self-discipline is fine. Needless to say, if you answered, "No, I seldom do those unpleasant things," your self-discipline may be too weak for successful risking. On the other hand, the problem may not be one of self-discipline but could instead be an unclear goal or a low level of commitment or motivation.

If you are highly motivated, self-discipline almost takes care of itself. Some people work better and faster if a deadline is glowering over the horizon; others prefer to pace themselves along the way without the need for last-minute spurts. Finding your own best approaches and sticking to them despite alluring distractions is the essence of self-discipline.

Self-esteem. You need to like yourself and feel that you have a right to succeed. You need to believe in yourself and your future, as well as to be able to see yourself getting ahead and enjoying it.

In the previous chapter, we helped you evaluate and improve your own self-esteem. So all we're doing here is to remind you of its importance.

Sense of adventure. Risk-taking demands getting out of a rut because ruts get too comfortable and lead nowhere. If you have a sense of adventure, you actively search for ways to grow and change; you're always willing to charge into new arenas if there is something you want to go for.

An active sense of adventure comes from taking the plunge successfully and/or learning that even failure is a way of learning and has its own rewards. You've never done it before? Well, you can't start any younger. Do it!

Sense of humor. To offset your self-esteem you need an ability to laugh at yourself and to avoid taking yourself too seriously. Being able to see the ridiculous and the bizarre all around you and letting go with a good belly laugh have saved many a risk-taker from despair.

True, you are more apt to be born with a sense of humor than to be able to develop one, but few people are completely humorless. Everyone has the opportunity to lighten up his or her viewpoint and avoid acting pompously.

Sense of Timing. Is this the best time to risk or should I wait? A sixth sense seems to be required sometimes to tell us when the time is right.

There is a time for giving up the old and moving on. The exact time varies with each person, of course, since each person is the sum of her experience and must move at her own pace. However, if you do not risk changing when the time is right, you may be forced to change when you are least prepared.

Don't waste time regretting your past or present life. No matter how bad it was or how you suffered, it was positive preparation to enable you to change now. Sometimes it takes enduring a difficult situation to show you what must be done. A whole load of discouragement may be the needed catalyst to make you give up self-destructive attitudes and habits.

Forget the knight on the white horse. Don't keep postponing your risk in the hope that someone will take you away from all this to the Land of Riskfree. Giving up this vain hope and accepting the idea that you can be your own agent for change heralds your march to maturity.

Many risks fail because they were either premature or not taken in time. Mary Ann knew that she should consider asking for another job. Since her position had been reclassified, she didn't seem to be getting anywhere and there wasn't enough work to keep her busy and interested. She kept hoping the situation would improve, but it didn't. She wanted more challenge, but was fearful about talking to her boss.

One afternoon she was called into the boss's office to be told that she was fired because she was inefficient. She tried to explain that the reclassification had taken the satisfaction out of her work and that she had wanted to talk to him about it. But it was too late; her last-ditch appeal didn't work. She had not risked asserting herself in time.

Take time to correct mistakes even when the act of risking is under way. If the people you thought would be supportive in your efforts turn out not to be, terminate that association as quickly as possible and move on. A good risk can be made better by compensating for the errors you discover.

Allow enough lead time to know what you are doing. Pre-

pare beforehand. Go through it in your mind's eye if you
can't experience it in fact. Imagine yourself there. What
would you do? What would you say? How would you react?
Merely setting your mind in the direction of your con-
templated risk is often all you need to become familiar with
what you feel.

When you've decided upon a risk, commit yourself to it. If
you delay at the moment of leaping, you can lose both your
momentum and your objective.

Rosalie decided to return to school after many years absence. She began by contacting school officials, exploring
curricula and courses of study, arranging for child care and,
most important, investigating scholarship possibilities. After
eight months of intensive effort, she secured a full scholarship, decided what she wanted to study, and found competent child care.

All factors were go when suddenly she slowed to a stop
because of self doubts. What if she couldn't develop good
study habits? Maybe the scholarship would be withdrawn.
Fear grabbed and inhibited her. She chose to retreat from her
former commitment and forfeited her future education as
well as her self-esteem.

Make a timetable for risking. You don't have to follow it
exactly, but a good schedule can be a persuasive force for
direction. It further reinforces the belief in the plan that
you're working on. Anything that enables you to pursue your
risk should be encouraged.

Avoid taking time out in the middle of risking. Focus your
energy on completing the risk. Get through the crisis before
giving yourself a break. Even a short recess at the wrong time
could cause you to lose momentum.

Improving your sense of timing can start with an awareness
that everything and everyone flows with time, at a certain

pace, at a unique rhythm. You can learn to know your own rhythm by spending a day or two alone, with no watches or clocks to govern you. Eat only when you're hungry, sleep only when you're tired. Another suggestion is to keep a diary or journal to indicate when you are highly energized and when you are blah. Are you a morning person? Do you only come alive after dark? Study your own timing and that of the other people involved in your risking situation and try to time what you do for the peak rather than the down times.

If you're afraid you won't know when the best time to risk occurs, it might be that you are not thoroughly enough prepared. Have you done your homework? Have you studied similar risking quests in terms of timing? Talk to people who were involved. How did they know when the time was right?

Winning Attitude. Winners go into any contest with the expectation that they are going to win. If you feel successful, you will act successfully. If you're new at risking, you may have to work at a winning attitude and psyche yourself up for the fray.

Alice was determined to change from a research job to a sales position in a large corporation. Several efforts failed but she never lost her winning attitude. Using another offer as leverage, she was finally accepted as a sales trainee, but she was told the transfer would mean a decrease in salary. Alice decided this wasn't fair, considering how long she had worked for the company in a staff position, so she approached her new boss determined to win.

As it turned out, Alice did not win the goal she had in mind—to maintain her present salary. But after the risk-taking interview she *felt* like a winner, and *was* because what she got instead was the use of a company car and the kind of schedule that would permit her to finish work on her Master's degree in Business Administration. She was able to come out a winner because she was smart enough to see that what was offered to her, although different from her original goal, was really better for her in the long run.

Alice, now a successful sales person, continues her winning ways. She says, for example, that whenever a potential customer has an objection, she refuses to consider it as a "No." Instead she treats each objection *as a request for more information*.

Developing a winning attitude should be the result of all the other factors. Since nothing succeeds like success, one small triumph will make you feel like a beginning winner and several favorable outcomes should make you feel like a real and consistent winner. What's important here, however—no matter what your track record is so far—is to work at being optimistic about your chances. If you expect to win, you have a psychological advantage.

Essential Knowledge and Skills

Assertiveness. Thanks to books and workshops, more and more women are learning how to assert themselves. Nevertheless, the behavior of some indicates that they don't know the difference between assertiveness and aggressiveness. Being assertive means stating clearly and firmly what you want (and why, if that information is appropriate) while aggressiveness means going after what you want by stepping on other people's toes. Women who conceal their feelings and go along with someone else's demands or requests to avoid taking a stand are not being either assertive or aggressive. They are being passive and what they probably think of as "nice."

For example, suppose a colleague wants to borrow your secretary for a backlog of work in his department. Normally, this would not be an unreasonable request, but right now you are fighting against a deadline for a project your boss has assigned, which, if done well and on time, could bring great reward to your department and to you. Here are three different responses you might make:

Nonassertive, wishy-washy: (in low, weak voice)	Well, I guess so if you really need her and think your work is more important.
Aggressive: (in loud, angry tones)	Hell, no! Just because you let your people get behind in their work, it's not my problem!
Assertive: (in a firm, positive manner)	I'm sorry I can't release her right now because we're in the middle of a crash project. But we should be through in about two days and then I'll be glad to make some of her time available.

There may be times when you feel like being aggressive and dumping on the other person. But consider the value of helping the other person see your position rather than your anger. Consider also the consequences of riding roughshod over someone that you may have to do business with again. Assertiveness is a skill that gets your ideas across without putting anyone down. Notice also, in the office example above, that the assertive response gives the other person an alternative instead of a flat no.

Communication Abilities. Successful risking can often depend upon your ability to communicate. How well do you speak and listen? Although our educational systems focus more heavily on reading and writing, we actually spend far more time every day listening and speaking. Unfortunately, many people today are self-taught listeners and speakers, having learned by imitation and trial and error. True, we couldn't function, let alone risk, if we could not speak and listen in some fashion. But consider this: research shows that most people listen at only 25 percent efficiency. This doesn't mean you missed 75 percent (although that may be true); it means that of what you heard, you correctly understood only *one-fourth!* That's a scary statistic when you recall how much of your education was in lecture form and when you think of all the dialogues and discussions in which you participate. Maybe some of what you firmly believe just isn't so!

Effective speaking depends more on clear organization of ideas than it does on pear-shaped tones of the "How, now, brown cow!" era. Getting ideas from your head to other people's heads is often a tricky business, however, because there are no meanings in the words we use, no matter how carefully we choose them. Words don't mean; people mean. So the goal of communication is to share as much meaning as possible and to do that we must constantly check the feedback we get. "Do I understand that the point you are making is . . ." is an excellent way to both give and get feedback rather than assume you completely understand the other person's viewpoint. This approach allows the other person to say either, "That's right" or, "No, that isn't quite what I meant. What I mean is . . ."

Nonverbal communication covers all those signs, signals, and nuances that go along with the words or instead of the words. A sarcastic tone of voice can change a positive meaning to negative or a bland statement to a humorous one. A booted and holstered policeman, swaggering down the sidewalk, doesn't have to say a word to send out a loud and clear message. Whether it is the message he intends to give is another matter.

Be careful, when risking, that you don't concentrate so hard on what you are saying that you overlook the nonverbal messages you are inadvertently sending. An inappropriate, perhaps unconscious smile, or stroking of your hair or neck could broadcast uncertainty.

In any two-person conversation, far more meaning is transmitted back and forth via nonverbal cues than the words themselves convey. In your moment of risk, are you aware of the underlying messages you are sending? And are these messages congruent with your words and what you intend to convey? If there is a contradiction between your words and your nonverbal signals, your listeners will believe the nonverbal because it appears to be more spontaneous and more honest.

In the next chapter we will discuss the value of knowing you look your best. For now, think about the message value in the way you dress, sound, and move. We do not suggest that you dress in a certain way because only you can determine what your intended message is and what effect your choice of clothing will have on you and on the people involved in your risking situation. Another reason why we reject the notion that there is a right way to dress is that, if this were true, we would all be wearing look-alike uniforms. Our only point here is that clothes and grooming communicate, whether we meant them to or not; let's make sure they are communicating what we want them to.

A psychologist we know has decided not to wear a light-blue suit on an airplane any more. She was asked for magazines by two different male passengers. We love her comeback: "I'm not the stewardess. I'm the pilot."

Communicating successfully requires that you care about other people. You must care about whether they are listening to you and understanding you and whether they find you a credible source of information. Do you demonstrate that you know what you're talking about and therefore have the right to be listened to? You must care about the speaker in order to listen well and resist distractions. Do you give other people your full listening attention or does your mind wander to what you want to say next? Do you hear the other person out before you reach conclusions and evaluate the worth of their comments?

If you aren't certain about your own abilities in communication or interpersonal transactions, one way to find out how you're doing is to ask for feedback from other people. You can do this in informal conversations or, more formally, by using a feedback form like the following. Select people who know you well and who will give you honest reactions, neither too severe nor too kind. These are only suggested feedback topics; change them to suit your own needs.

GOALS FOR PERSONAL DEVELOPMENT

Please help me set my personal/professional goals for development by giving me feedback on this form. Based on my relationship with you and others, mark each item to indicate whether you think I'm doing all right, need to improve, need to do more, or need to do less. Some goals that are not listed may be more important for me than those listed so please write any additional goals on the blank lines. Finally, please go over the whole list and circle the numbers of the three or four activities which you feel are the most important for me to work on. Thank you._____

(sign your name here)

	DOING ALL RIGHT	NEED TO IMPROVE	NEED TO DO MORE	NEED TO DO LESS
Communication skills:				
1. Amount of talking	_____	_____	_____	_____
2. Listening alertly	_____	_____	_____	_____
3. _____	_____	_____	_____	_____
Observation skills:				
4. Sensing others' feelings	_____	_____	_____	_____
5. Noting reaction to me	_____	_____	_____	_____
6. _____	_____	_____	_____	_____
Problem-solving skills:				
7. Evaluating ideas critically	_____	_____	_____	_____
8. Clarifying issues	_____	_____	_____	_____
9. Summarizing	_____	_____	_____	_____
10. _____	_____	_____	_____	_____
Morale-building skills:				
11. Harmonizing, helping people reach agreement	_____	_____	_____	_____
12. Upholding rights of individuals under group pressure	_____	_____	_____	_____
13. _____	_____	_____	_____	_____
Emotional expressiveness:				
14. Being authentic	_____	_____	_____	_____
15. Being tactful	_____	_____	_____	_____
16. _____	_____	_____	_____	_____
Ability to handle emotional situations:				
17. Ability to face conflict, anger	_____	_____	_____	_____
18. Ability to stand tension	_____	_____	_____	_____
19. _____	_____	_____	_____	_____
Other:				
20. _____	_____	_____	_____	_____
21. _____	_____	_____	_____	_____

Communication can usually be studied in regular or adult education classes at local universities or community colleges. You'll find it included in classes called "Communication" or "Speech." Other relevant classes might be "Group Discussion," "Argumentation and Logic," or "Persuasion." Any or all of these subjects are worth studying in order to improve your general communication effectiveness.

Decision Making and Problem Solving. Both decision making and problem solving are processes in which we all engage but to do them well takes thought, knowledge, and practice. We must make decisions when we have to make a choice. Shall I ask for that raise now or later? Shall I buy the green suit or the brown one? Our decisions may be made on impulse, without thought; then after we have made our choice, we try to think of all the reasons why it was a good thing to do. Of course, this is rationalizing after the fact. Far better to do our thinking first so that the choices we make will be based on evidence and thoughtful consideration rather than impulse.

Problem solving is more complicated. In this process we make many decisions on the way from locating and defining the problem to selecting the best solution out of those we were able to generate. Maybe you use the traditional approach involving specific steps and reflective thinking. Or perhaps you like the nontraditional where you enter the aspects of the problem in your think tank and then wait for the inspiration or the *gestalt* flash in which the solution shimmers up out of your subconscious. Either process can work very well as can a combination of the two.

Regardless of your chosen method, the point is that problems are best solved when they have been thoroughly thought through first. What is wrong that appears in need of change? Finding the problem's key may be the most difficult task of all. For example, if you go out to start your car in the morning and it won't start, what is your problem? Many people would make the mistake of thinking their problem is to get the car started, but that is a solution, not a problem. Your problem is to find transportation to get to work. Getting the car fixed is one possibility, but calling a cab, taking the bus, or hitching a ride are all potentially better solutions if you are pressed for time.

Once you know what your problem really is, next go to work on its causes and its history. Suppose your problem is your need to improve a working relationship with a colleague with whom you always seem to be at odds. When did the trouble start? What are the symptoms? Does his behavior have a pattern to it or occur the same way all the time? Does the person have conflicts with other employees or just you? The more information you can ferret out, the better will be the solution you eventually evolve.

After background analysis, some people want to leap right into suggesting solutions, but a better thing to do at this stage is to establish some criteria. How will you know when you have found the best solution? Checking against your pre-established criteria is an effective technique. For example, if you want to buy a house, you wouldn't just charge off looking at any and all houses for sale, would you? First you would decide such things as your price bracket, the number of bedrooms you need, the kind of neighborhood you want, your needs for transportation, schools, and so forth. Some of these criteria would probably be on your must list while others would be nice to have but could be done without if necessary.

Now you're ready for dreaming up solutions to your problem. Advocates of brainstorming and the creative approach say you should not stop with just one or two potential solutions, because not only the more the merrier, but also the more the better quality. The fifteenth idea is usually better than the earlier ones. Last, you look over all your solutions and pick the best one and put it into action.

Risk-takers need to know how best to make decisions and solve problems. If you lack skill in these areas, you may find yourself risking unnecessarily or trying to solve the wrong problem. Look before you risk, and above all, think it all the way through.

Organization. The ability to organize can't be separated from the thinking process. Each time we put ideas into a sequence we have to understand their relationship. Because we have to think through every stage, putting similar materials together and outlining represent exercises in logic.

The first and most important goal of organization is to turn a conglomeration into something unified and balanced. Organized ideas are far easier to deal with than a hodgepodge.

Let's assume you have been asked to give a report to a club meeting on the Hospice Movement in the United States. Where do you begin? Perhaps at the beginning with the history of hospices first in England and then in this country. Or perhaps you could confine your information to a description of the hospice organization nearest you. Other possibilities would be comparing different hospices or confining yourself to anecdotal information about people who have been served by hospice volunteers.

The point is that you first have to *think through* the possibilities, *make choices,* and then *plan* for the best sequence of ideas. This is the process of organizing.

Successful riskers are not only well organized, they *look* organized. We have been talking primarily about organizing ideas, but lives and closets need organizing, too. If your briefcase is neatly arranged and you are able to pull out the precise document you need when you need it, you have sent a powerful message to the people you're dealing with.

Summary

Getting your rear in gear requires a commitment to action. You can confirm that you're ready to risk by making sure you either already have or are working on acquiring the essential qualities and attitudes along with the essential knowledge and skills. Don't despair if you come up short on your inventory; help is available.

FOUR

KEEPING FIT FOR SUCCESSFUL

RISKING

CALCULATED risking is a mandate for a dynamic life. Yet each risking task requires a new source of energy. Where does your vitality come from? What are your energy needs? Some of the energy sources we will look at in this chapter and in other parts of the book are: *goals, motivation, commitment, wellness, creativity, attitudes, appearance,* and *environment.*

Source of Energy

Goals. It's hard to be "up" for a task or a risk without a clear purpose. Mountain and rock climbers may have their eyes on the next crack for a toehold, but their mental image is of the top. So it is with risking.

Knowing your overall purpose for risking helps you focus on the tasks at hand and plan your risks accordingly. If you don't have a clear picture of your risk objective, you won't be able to distinguish between winning and losing.

Confusion can surround any discussion of goals and objectives because people mean different things by these terms. For clarity's sake, we ask you to accept our definitions:

Purpose: Your overall aim—where you'd like to be ten or twenty years from now and what you'd like to accomplish by then.

Goals: Specific targets with timetables—those interim steps you plan to take in the next one, two, or three years to help you achieve your purpose. Goals should be measurable so you'll know when you've reached them.

Objectives: Steps to take to reach your goals—what needs to be done to help you get there.

For specific examples of how objectives, goals, and purpose fit together, see Chapter Eight, where we work through the process for such situations as preparing yourself for a better job or becoming president of a volunteer agency's board of directors.

Because goal setting seems like hard work, the process is too often ignored or postponed. But if you don't know where you're going, how do you know when you get there? Effective risk-takers not only set goals, they do it conscientiously *in writing* and revise and update their targets regularly.

Aim for something realistic and achievable. Some women fail because they expect too much of themselves and want to be perfect, or they continually postpone risking until all circumstances are ideal. Waiting for perfection is an endless, pointless occupation. And we agree with George Bernard Shaw when he wrote:

> People are always blaming their circumstances for what they are. I don't believe in circumstances. The people who get on in this world are the people who get up and look for the circumstances they want, and, if they can't find them, make them.

Promise yourself that you won't put off your own goal setting any longer. Set some modest aims first for practice and see what happens. It works!

Motivation. As we said in the previous chapter, the impetus that stirs you to activity, the force that pushes you toward getting what you want, is motivation. When your actions become purposeful and your life begins to make sense, energy comes from your degree of motivation. For many women, when they center their minds on an objective worth risking for, no fear of risking or reluctance to risk can hold them back. The risk itself provides the motivation and consequent energy.

Commitment. When risking, you are the actress playing center stage in your own life drama. While nonriskers watch impotently from the wings, you write and star in your own script. A prime source of energy is your degree of commitment to controlling your own life and destiny. Feeling helpless and blaming fate or others do not produce energy. Commitment to reaching your goals and to risking for them produces high energy.

Effective risk-takers do not commit themselves blindly to just any risk, however. Their commitment to risk and to follow through comes only after they have done their homework and calculated the odds.

Your first commitment should be to do something about the situation that has you uptight and miserable. Promise yourself to quit procrastinating.

Your next commitment should be to yourself. Peggy was one woman who had to learn this truth the hard way by denying her own needs and worth until it was almost too late.

It seemed to her that she had always worked, starting as a teenager, waitressing and babysitting after school to supplement her blue-collar family's income. She married early, produced three sons, and went right on working, this time in her husband's furniture store. And her very handsome husband never let her forget that he was something and she was nothing.

Then one day her husband left her for another woman.

But Peggy's life hardly changed. More work. Just one less person to pick up after.

She took over ownership of the store and supplemented her income by making custom draperies at night. Despite her strength, determination, and ability to survive, Peggy's self-esteem continued to sag. And still her life was bounded by unending hard work.

Then, glory be, just as the fairy tales say, she met and quickly married a very wealthy man. At last! She could finally take it easy and spend quality time with her sons. Her newfound spare time led her to renew an old love, sports. She began biking and running and also joined a swim team. "Everything was going my way," she said, "but I was still downtrodden and unhappy."

Peggy sought out a counselor and, with her help, soon saw that the second marriage for money rather than love was a mistake and that the only way she could build her self-esteem was to do something for herself and on her own.

When last seen, Peggy had set and reached the goal of completing a grueling triathalon. Even though she was over forty years old, she finished all three events—biking, swimming, and running a marathon.

She has no self-esteem problems now. "I believe in myself," Peggy said triumphantly. "I'm planning to start my own, sports-oriented business and enter another triathalon. Life has so much challenge and meaning! I don't want to miss a moment!"

Peggy's life took a dramatic turnaround when she figured out that what she had lacked was commitment to herself.

Wellness. We strongly believe in the concept of holistic health, in which the mind and the body are inseparable and people use their own powers to take an active role in the promotion of their own health and well-being. Our body/minds are continually giving us feedback and information to improve our diets and exercise programs, and to find the most appropriate balance between activity and rest, but many of us ignore the feedback. Wellness practitioners work to open the channels of communication between the part of us that is giving the feedback and the part of us that is designed to listen to that feedback and respond to it. To test this out, eat whatever you want, whenever you want, and then tune in to the feedback your body/mind will give you.

Since we are the products of our own minds, the only person who prevents us from actualizing our full potential is ourself. When we nourish ourselves with the highest thoughts, we develop a positive self-image which, as we have said, is a necessary tool for successful risking.

Three energy sources that are also vital to wellness are *rest and relaxation*, *exercise*, and *diet*. Rest and relaxation are genuine energizers. Letting go of the tension in the muscles and the mind allows the body to replenish itself. Physical exercise is another way to both achieve relaxation and acquire energy. A regular program of racketball, aerobic dancing, hiking, or jogging creates and replenishes energy. Finally, the body's chief energy source is the food we eat. Food and drink are quite literally the fuels that keep us going. Wise choices of the kinds and amounts of what we put in our mouths can create and conserve our energy.

Health is not limited to the absence of disease, but includes a fully active life of joy, productivity, a sense of purpose, and a spirit of love. Each of us has a greater role to play in our health or illness than many of us have previously been willing to acknowledge. We can take control of our lives and our health if we really want to. When dis-stress, dis-ease, or dis-order occur, something is abnormal. Such a deviation from the norm usually indicates a belief system with self-limiting thoughts, negative self-images, and distorted attitudes that have interfered with the balanced functioning of nature.

Creativity. There is an enormous reservoir of talent and creativity in all of us. Creativity blossoms when you are intensely involved with someone or something. Can you recall the last time you lost yourself in an activity? When you lost all track of time and forgot to eat or sleep? When the creative juices are flowing, energy abounds. You are on an emotional and physical high.

When you are creatively absorbed in something, you experience a positive kind of stress. The quickened heartbeat, higher blood pressure, increased constriction of vision, becoming oblivious to the passage of time and the things around you, add up to optimal stress. Creativity has its genesis in this threshold of stress. You are open to explore new possibilities and acquire new insights. This is the point at which symphonies are composed, books are written, contracts are signed, races are won.

Creativity and originality are among the greatest resources a person can have with which to face life. Many times when we are confronted with crises, we tend to retreat to a known and secure strategy. Yet these are the very times when a new approach is most needed.

For example, when you are in a love relationship and have risked exposing your emotions and needs and have been rejected, you might fall back on those old feelings of low self-worth. You feel unlovable and that there is no tomorrow. A more original—and healing—approach would be to take yourself in hand and acknowledge that this is a painful experience but that there is merit in growing through pain. Tell yourself that new awareness, sensitivity, and strength are bound to come from your courage in facing the problem.

Remind yourself that you have loved before and you will love again.

Attitudes. At the risk of sounding like Pollyanna, we feel we cannot overemphasize the importance and value of a positive attitude. Developing a winning attitude creates energy, whereas a defeatist position creates a self-fulfilling prophesy. Energy comes from bouncing back. When you're handed a lemon, make lemonade.

If you study the ways of successful risk-takers who get what they want from life, you will see that they conduct themselves positively with others. When they enter a room and greet people, the message they give is "Hello! There you are!" rather than "Here I am." They communicate their appreciation and acceptance of you as you are; they refrain from judging or responding in a negative way. They seek out points of agreement and are able to build on these to reduce the separations between you.

Knowing You Look Good. Chances are that a sampling of 100 women would reveal that 99 are dissatisfied with some aspect of their appearance. Women who otherwise look like fashion models will privately complain about overweight or underweight, about inadequate cheekbones or a nose that is too long or too short. Is it a part of the condition of being female to find fault with ourselves?

Let's vow to reform and rid ourselves of this unrealistic perfectionism. Let's analyze ourselves in the mirror and all agree that we aren't half bad-looking. If some of the areas that lack perfection can be changed, let's get to work. If the so-called fault is built in, let's forget about it after doing what we can to minimize it. But most of all, let's emphasize and make the most of all those good points we know we have.

A wardrobe consultant told us that the most common mistake women make is not to change their style as they grow older. Not realizing that they have outgrown a particular look, some women make unfavorable choices that express the way they were five or ten years ago. Dress should express a personality, a lifestyle, what a person does, but also that person's age.

Some women are still wearing harsh, bright makeup that is no longer flattering because their own coloring has softened with age. Others still buy clothes in the size they used to wear, regardless of fit.

Here are two helpful suggestions:

1. Go through magazines (general publications, not fashion or beauty magazines) and study the photographs for appearances that appeal to you and those that don't. Select three or four to cut out. Analyze what it is in the positive pictures that attracts you so strongly. Try to detect the inner quality that the clothing and coloring express. Then go through your own wardrobe to see if you are expressing your own inner quality in the way that you want.

2. Find two photographs of yourself, one that you like and one that you don't like. Analyze the main factors in both pictures. Try to devise ways to improve the factors you don't like and highlight those you do.

If you aren't sure how to emphasize your good points, paying for advice and counsel on the uses of makeup and clothing styles and colors is money well spent. Positive energy comes from knowing you look your best. When you are confident that you are making a good impression, you have energy left over for total risking.

Environment. What kind of an environment offers and preserves energy? You have to identify your own needs and arrange to meet them.

Some people like to have a sign on their desk that says, "A

cluttered desk is the mark of genius." Do clutter and apparent disorganization give you energy or take it away? If you decide that a lack of organization is hampering you, then cleaning out your place by discarding, giving away, or selling anything that is not essential is good business and good therapy. Provide an environment that pleases and satisfies you.

A Chicago mother wanted to have her own business but was homebound because of her large family. She reorganized her home and now has her own secretarial and answering service. At first she found the only quiet place to work was the bathroom, so she set up her office equipment there.

Your environment, quiet or noisy, cluttered or spartan, well lighted or dim, can set either a positive or negative stage for your efforts. It all depends on you.

Analyze your own sources of energy by writing down the answers to the following questions:

What daily experiences are sources of energy?

What people provide nourishment and strength?

How often do I call them when I feel down and need a lift?

Can I mentally get in touch with my flow of energy?

Can I recall the excitement that generates energy?

What activity (such as walking, running, dancing) gets my energy flowing?

Who views me as a source of energy and why?

How much of my time is spent in low-energy pursuits?

How much of my energy do I invest in thinking, feeling, doing?

Which are my major and minor goals right now?

Which ones energize me?

Do I reward myself for doing what I need to accomplish?

Do I set aside time to be with high-energy people?

Do I believe in myself and my power to bring about change?

What foods are energy sources for me?

Do I believe I have energy enough to take the necessary risks to reach my goals?

What kinds of energy do I need for risking?

Energy Depleters

What drains you of energy? What, or whom, should you avoid? When are you at your best and raring to go? When do you feel ninety-nine years old?

Obviously, you can identify energy depleters by returning to the energy sources we have just discussed and examining their flip sides. You lose energy if you lack goals, motivation, commitment, and so on. In addition to these, there are three more energy depleters you should be warned against.

First, taking too many risks at once can produce mental, physical, and emotional exhaustion, as well as creative burnout. One woman we interviewed found herself in the middle of a divorce and child-custody conflict that necessitated her moving into a different house. A new man entered her life and demanded attention. At this most inopportune time, her job was phased out and she had to begin a search for a new one. She has managed to come through these multiple crises but she would not recommend that anyone else demonstrate such a poor sense of timing. One risk at a time is plenty, particularly for beginners.

Second, what may appear to be conviction and perseverance in some turns out to be sheer stubbornness in others. Holding on when the risk seems overwhelming or destined to fail falls in the stubbornness category. You can usually tell if something isn't going to work. If that is the case, drop it. Let a bad risk have its demise. Don't waste your precious energy on a lost cause.

Third, what about the people in your life? An interesting

and highly revealing activity is to list all the people in your life that you regularly spend time with. Then note which of these people give you energy and which drain your energy. What does this tell you? For one thing, avoid the energy drainers on a high-risk day!

Rechanneling Stress into Energy

Under the daily pressures of today's fast-paced lifestyles, uncontrolled tension diminishes daily accomplishments and wastes energy, as well as being harmful to your health. Since we cannot hope to totally eliminate the pressures of life, it's important to learn how to understand them and deal with them.

Stress has acquired a bad image, probably because the term was borrowed from physics and engineering, where the meaning is precise: the application of sufficient force to an object or system to distort or deform it. Perhaps this original meaning has kept us thinking too long in terms of forces outside ourselves.

In the human body, however, stress is not always precise and sometimes it isn't even recognized. Events in themselves do not produce stress reactions. What creates overt stress is how we perceive and react to the events. For example, one person may thoroughly enjoy traveling to Europe alone; another might find the uncertainty of being alone as well as coping with different lifestyles and cultures extremely stressful.

Stress can be your powerful ally. Dealing with stress is a matter of self-direction. You can use the power of your inner resources to develop a state of harmony and balance within your body and your mind.

Three Kinds of Stress. 1. *Stress underload* is characterized by boredom and comes from such situations as being overqualified for your job. There is no challenge, no excitement. Apathy, accidents, absenteeism, undereating or overeating, negativity, lethargy, irritability, and dullness are all symptomatic.

2. *Stress overload* occurs when a person's energies are overextended and she is in a state of near exhaustion and burnout. An overextended organism creates irritability, insomnia, alcoholism, absenteeism, indecisiveness, and withdrawal. Stress overload is the underlying cause of many major illnesses such as cancer, high blood pressure, and heart attacks.

3. *Optimal stress* happens when you stand on the threshold of stress, but feel exhilarated, highly motivated, mentally alert. Your perceptions are sharp, you are calm under pressure, and your energy levels are high. As we noted previously, this is the kind of positive stress which makes great achievements possible.

Try a "Hassle Log." To find out how you ride the stress express, try keeping a hassle log. For at least two weeks, keep track of the tensions and joys that happen to you from the time you get up in the morning until you go to bed at night.

SAMPLE HASSLE LOG

List of tensions	Where, doing what	Thoughts, feelings	Response
1. Tightness in stomach. Headache.	At home. Late. Rushing to get to work.	Frustration. Anxiety. "I'm late again and always behind."	Hurry more.

At the end of two weeks, add another category. Put down your ideal response or how you would like to respond to the situation. Try the new behavior and see if there isn't a positive difference in your response to daily tension.

Rest and Relaxation. Tension disorders are fatigue producers and energy drainers. When you are fearful or anxious, you set the stage for nervous indigestion, spastic colon, high blood pressure, or a peptic ulcer. However, when you relax muscles and experience complete absence of movement in your body, you liberate new sources of physical and psychic strength. You gain more power to do what you need to do with your life.

When you want to relax, take deep breaths and feel the oxygen surging through your body. The more oxygen dispersal, the greater the sense of relaxation. When you are tense, the first thing that happens is that your breathing becomes shallow. As oxygen to the brain diminishes, thinking and concentration become difficult. When muscles are deprived of oxygen, they become tight.

Breathe in to the count of three, breathe out to the count of three. Establish a comfortable rhythm that sets the pace for harmony throughout your body.

As you breathe in, begin to stretch. Reach your arms up to the ceiling and imagine you are pushing against it. Then reach out to the left and right, as if you were pushing against the walls. Then drop, like a rag doll, and allow tight muscles to become slack.

Autogenic Training for Relaxation. When you want to experience a more complete form of relaxation, try the autogenic method. Do it daily for from six to ten minutes, preferably at a regular time so that you condition your body. When that regular time arrives, such as before or after lunch, your body will automatically respond with a release of tension.

1. Lie down on a firm surface or sit in a straight chair in rag-doll fashion, feet flat on the floor, spine relaxed, hands or

arms resting on the thighs. Close your eyes.

2. Direct your attention to the particular body part and say the appropriate phrase several times.

3. "My right arm is heavy." (If you are left-handed, say the left arm.) Think strongly about the heaviness in your arm. Remember the heavier the body part, the stronger the relaxation ability.

4. Say: "I am completely calm."

5. Continue to concentrate on a particular body part and say: "My right leg is heavy." "My left leg is heavy." "My neck and shoulders are heavy."

6. Concentrate again on the body part. This time say: "My right arm is warm."

7. Repeat several times each: "My right leg is warm." "My left leg is warm." "My neck and shoulders are heavy."

8. "My breathing is calm, I am relaxed."

9. Mentally repeat: "My forehead is cool."

At the end of six to ten minutes, depending upon your ability to concentrate, slowly stretch your arms up above your head, flex your feet, and gently sit or stand up.

A key principle of the theory of autogenic training is that the body will balance itself when directed into a relaxed state. Optimal balance, or homeostasis, is brought about by the practice of autogenic training. The benefits that result are:

1. Tensions are reduced and concentration is increased.

2. Sleep disturbances are effectively minimized.

3. Self-confidence builds as you realize that it is one area of your life where you are in full control.

4. Daily problems are neutralized as relaxation is increased. You can develop an attitude of detachment that helps you more efficiently reach a resolution.

5. This exercise increases peripheral blood flow, relaxes the blood vessels, and promotes self-healing physiological changes.

Eating for Energy

Good nutrition to increase your vitality and rejuvenative processes emphasizes foods that have the greatest amount of aliveness. The best foods are those grown in the sun, the site of energy, and which are closer to their natural states. For example, raw fresh fruits and vegetables are more nourishing than cooked foods that have vitamins and minerals steamed out. In addition, raw foods are digested more slowly, enabling the body to assimilate and send nutriments to the vital organs more quickly.

Besides raw fresh fruits and vegetables, other alive foods are yogurts, and seeds such as those from pumpkin, sesame, and sunflower. Brewer's yeast is the best source of B complex and some trace minerals. Sprouts and grains are also energy foods.

Low-fat protein sources are baked and broiled chicken, turkey, or fish. Low-fat cheeses are Edam, cottage cheese, ricotta, and farmer's cheese. Easy to digest are watercress, green beans, bananas, whey bran, lecithin, apricots, apple juice, brussel sprouts, cabbage, cauliflower, cherries, and cranberries.

If you have to eat on the run, consider a high-protein drink like this one made in a blender: To one cup of juice or buttermilk add one tablespoon each of brewer's yeast, protein powder, whey, and pieces of fruit. If you like it with more zing, add one teaspoon of vanilla extract to cut the taste of the yeast. Not only is this drink an energizer, it's the best fatigue-fighter going.

Linda is a lovely woman who tried for several years to become a Hollywood star. Her Hispanic background gave her a beautiful face and figure but also a tendency to overweight from a diet of beans and enchiladas. She put all her waitressing income into voice and acting lessons and never missed an opportunity to audition.

While pushing herself harder and harder, Linda changed her diet to California junk food, eating only occasionally and on the run. True, she lost weight. But she also lost all her energy, until one day she was near collapse.

She took stock and changed both her diet and her career for the better. She began eating raw fruit and vegetables and protein snacks and began to prepare for a profession in the health field.

"I feel great!" Linda exclaimed. "What a difference a good diet makes!"

Reduce Stress with a High-Energy Diet. During times of overt stress and risking it is important to conserve what energy you have and replenish energy that is lost. This can be done with a diet for energy and stress reduction which includes a protein breakfast, light lunch, and moderate dinner. When you have a good breakfast, you are prepared, physically and emotionally, for your day's work. The brain will be clearer, and productivity will be greater. It will be possible to get through the day with a minimum of fatigue because the body is nutritionally sustained. There is truth to the old saying that we should "eat breakfast like a king, lunch like a peasant, and dinner like a pauper."

Parasitic foods that drain energy such as white bread, white flour, sugar, jams, cake, bacon, instant cereal, liquor, and coffee should be eliminated to reduce stress. Soothe hunger pangs with skim milk, an orange, or a wedge of cheese. Drinking two glasses of skim milk daily not only provides calcium that fights stress directly, but also washes the harmful by-products of metabolism out of the body.*

---

*For more information about stress, rest, and nutrition, read Betsy Morscher, *Heal Yourself the European Way* (New York: Parker Publishing Co., 1980).

Moving for Energy

If you want to prepare for a risk, get out of your chair and move around. Go for a walk. Do a dance routine in your living room. We used to think that exercise made us tired; now we know that exercise gives us energy and reduces stress. Try it. The next time you come home dog tired, go for a walk instead of heading for your recliner, and see if your energy level doesn't perk up.

Some women have found that if they take some kind of physical risk, such as going on an Outward Bound type of trip, or floating down a wild river, or camping at the North Pole, the personal and professional risks get easier. Now that sport classes and programs are more open to young girls, physical risking will no longer be so alien to women. Just think! It was only in 1984 that the Olympics included a women's marathon for the first time.

"Each critical aspect of life is conceived with movement; the organization of movement is central to everything we do." So says Dr. Moshe FeldenKrais, renowned Israeli scientist and founder of the process called Functional Integration and Awareness Through Movement, which is based on the idea that relearning how to move as we were intended to move leads to freedom to choose the most efficient and healthy organization of ourselves. The unbalanced can become balanced and the disordered ordered.

One woman who experienced a FeldenKrais Guild workshop was initially bored with the slow movement process designed to repattern brain activity, but she stuck it out for three days. By the last day she felt a sense of relaxation and clarity of thinking and went home to make big changes in her life. One vow was to give up her sitting-down job and get into a profession that required more activity.

If you avoid risk, it may be because you also avoid keeping

physically active. The less you move, the less able you are to move. Sedentary people are seldom the riskers of the world.

Summary

Risking requires energy and wellness. Aspects such as motivation and commitment are energy sources and their absence energy depleters. Stress can be a positive source when it is channeled into productive energy. Rest and relaxation, exercise, and appropriate diet all reduce stress, improve well-being, and keep you fit for successful risking.

FIVE

EMBRACING THE ALIEN
WITH ENTHUSIASM

WOULD you run up to a stranger and throw your arms around him or her, especially if the stranger looked downright odd, as if from another planet? Of course you wouldn't. So how is it that's what we're suggesting risk-takers should do? Stand by and we'll tell you.

The stranger we are talking about is the unknown at the other end of your risk. People are just naturally more fearful and suspicious of the unknown. But unwarranted fear and suspicion can only hold them back. What we are advocating is to make friends with the unknown and when its shape becomes clear to you through your risking experiences, go ahead and embrace that alien phenomenon with great enthusiasm. Why? Because that critter is your friend.

Welcome the Unknown

Successful risk-takers do not equate the unknown with evil or as something to be shunned. Instead they think and feel about it in terms of excitement, mystery, and a welcome change. Be advised that all important progress and innovation have been dependent upon people being willing to accept risk and enter the realm of the unknown. Unpredictability is the inevitable price of progress. We fear things in proportion to our ignorance of them.

Futurists are predicting that our culture will gradually give up its emphasis on science, carefully tested methods, and only those phenomena that can be measured. New, unexplored realms (within the human brain, for example) where exact measurement is difficult, are going to replace our preoccupation with the technical and the industrial. It is an exciting time in which to live and risk.

As we have said before, change and transition are inevitable aspects of living. When they are coupled with uncertainty, they cause us to twist and turn, to wonder, to shift, to squirm. Do I really want to change careers? Do I really want to confront the president of the club about her mismanagement? Do I really want to go through all the pain of a divorce? Risk-takers must look at change and transition in positive terms, as times for further self-exploration and experimentation.

Which Are the Most Alien Risks for Women?

Fortunately, we've come a long way since a woman's greatest risk was to get pregnant. In 1915, for example, women were seventy times more likely to die in childbirth than they are now.

No doubt each of us would rate our scariest risk, so far, quite differently. For some, moving to a new part of the country would be Number One, while for others, having to make cold calls for jobs or sales would rank right up there.

Unless they were accustomed to risking and had many successes behind them, however, the women we interviewed found the following risks to be the most difficult:

Being hurt
Admitting being hurt
Entering new love relationships
Ending unsatisfactory love relationships

Reaching for high or higher jobs or offices
Starting or changing a career
Changing a lifestyle
Starting or buying a business
Going back to school

Let's look at each of these in more detail.

Risking Being Hurt. "I'm not going to see Larry any more," Ruth said. Her friend asked why. "Because he's in the Army and he might get sent overseas. What if I fell in love with him and he got killed?" Ruth, like many women, was troubled by the "what-ifs." If you try to protect yourself from possible events, your life becomes more and more restricted. "What if the plane should crash?" results in cancelling an important business opportunity. "What if I can't learn how to study again?" means perpetual postponement of education.

Women are basically thought of as the vulnerable sex, needing protection and security. Although we are slowly changing that image, some of us still hang back from risking because we *might* get hurt. It's easier not to try than to try with the possibility of failing.

Trying to ward off being hurt also closes off your availability to joy and excitement and all the good emotions. Allowing yourself to be vulnerable to possible hurt lifts horizons and options. The best approach is to say to yourself, "I may get hurt; I may lose out. But I bet I'll learn from the experience and, no matter what, I can make something positive out of it."

Risking Admitting Being Hurt. If you are fearful that you will lose a friend or lover if you honestly share your feelings, ask yourself what you would really lose? Real friends care about your feelings. When hurt is unexpressed, it becomes anger. Telling a person who has hurt you that you are hurt is crucial to your emotional well-being and to an honest relationship.

True, when you admit your hurt feelings to others you run the risk of wounding them. But sound relationships require open and authentic communication. Expressing your hurt tactfully and in a caring way will open the door to deeper understanding.

Connie met Malcolm at an office party. He was an outside consultant who was finishing up work with her company. Soon they began socializing and Connie appreciated the opportunity to get out and away from the heavy demands her work made on her time and energy.

She enjoyed Malcolm's broad range of interests and knowledge. Little by little she became aware that his needs and wishes always came first. If she wanted to go dancing and he wanted to go to a movie, he would insist on his choice. For the sake of peace, Connie would give in. If he had a problem he insisted that she listen but turned off her need to discuss something by calling the subject petty.

As time went by, Malcolm was more and more frequently asking to borrow things—from books to money to her car. When she finally confessed she was getting uncomfortable with their one-way relationship, Malcolm exploded with, "If you aren't capable of giving in a relationship, then I don't want to see you any more."

Connie was deeply hurt. She had liked being with Malcolm but had to honestly admit he was no friend. Later she was able to look back on her tardy expression of being hurt as partly her own fault. The experience taught her to be more assertive and honest in her future communicating.

Risking Entering New Love Relationships. Among the greatest risks are those related to love. Falling in love is something like stepping off a cliff and hoping for something to break your fall. Some people try to protect themselves by entering love as though it were a game of cards involving all kinds of rules. But love is irrational, an intuitive emotional plunge involving nothing but uncertainty. Trying to control another's response or trying to make him or her play by the rules are futile endeavors.

Some women cannot make a commitment to another person until they can make a commitment to themselves. Others are unwilling to take risks of love because they feel that no one has ever loved them without reservations or conditions and no one ever will.

To love means to trust and trusting makes you vulnerable. Love is very, very chancy. You can never really be sure how long a relationship will last. The person you trust today may not be there tomorrow. Lovers fear getting too close, being rejected, or losing independence.

To keep a relationship alive there must be a continuous willingness to work through obstacles and misunderstandings. Being willing to reach out rather than holding back is vital.

Since people change and grow, there is always the risk that you won't grow in the same direction or at the same rate. If each person sees the other as unique and special, however, then how and when they grow can be accepted as sources of love rather than instigators for separation and growing apart.

Most people are ambivalent about wanting both closeness and distance; we want to be our own person, yet we also want intimate connection with someone else. It takes working through these contradictions with open communication to keep a relationship viable.

Love, like happiness, seldom arrives on schedule but at times when we least expect it. When we are taken by surprise, we are delighted but confused because we have to change all those plans we thought were so important.

For example, Bridget was a business consultant en route to

Washington to present a program at a national conference. Her two children were traveling with her because the three had planned a holiday after the conference. On the airplane, Bridget met a man whom she instantly felt drawn to and he to her. When she discovered he was attending the same conference and had reservations at the same hotel, she was delighted. He asked her to dinner that night and the two of them, plus her children, were together every night during the conference.

She felt a magnetic attraction and found herself thinking of him constantly. They were obviously being swept up into a special relationship, but she kept saying to herself, "A new relationship just isn't on my agenda right now. I don't have time for an involvement. Between the kids and my consulting business, my life is already too crowded."

Bridget decided that the attachment she felt to the man would probably fade with distance and, after she returned home, she tried to put him out of her mind. She concentrated on work and home. But the man called and she returned the call and the bond did not go away. She decided to risk opening up, trusting, and being completely genuine with her new love. She found that listening to her feelings and responding to him, even though he wasn't on her agenda, paid off. They are now happily together since he has relocated in her city.

Questions to ask yourself before entering a relationship:

What do I expect to get out of this relationship?

Do I accept the other person, or do I have a hidden agenda for changing him to my own specifications?

Does he accept me just as I am, with faults as well as virtues?

Will I communicate honestly or hold back and create barriers?

Will he open up to me as well?

Is this person really special to me or just someone to fill lonely hours?

What is the potential for growth? Can we each grow at our own level as well as grow together? Can we accept the personal difference in growth?

Do I like as well as love him?

Am I happier when we are together?

Can I honor my own needs for privacy as well as togetherness?

Could I handle it if he left?

Could I risk loving again should this relationship end?

Risking Ending Unsatisfactory Love Relationships. When two people are no longer special to one another, when honesty is compromised, when intimacy and sharing are no longer present, then love is on the wane. When unfulfilled needs from a past relationship are placed on a present one, you cannot expect it to survive. Yet many of us hang on, hoping for improvement, long past any rational timing.

At the time a deep and loving relationship ends, you probably feel rejected, sorry for yourself, miserable. Your self-esteem slips ten notches; you wallow in depression. We've all been there. Fear of experiencing these feelings has often been the only thread holding an unsatisfactory relationship together. Learning to call a halt, learning when to say goodbye, require strength and determination. If you are to learn from the experience, you must grit your teeth and do it and not fall back into habitual responses.

Being able to say, "I will never return to that situation again," can be a source of strength and a resolution of commitment. Understanding what went wrong (It can't be *all* his fault!) will help you evaluate your decision and also keep you from leaping immediately into a similar situation.

Healing will take place in three predictable stages. First will come shock-denial, next hurt, anger, and depression, followed at last by acceptance and understanding. It's important to realize that a new chapter in your life has begun and to think of beginnings, not endings. You can make new love happen by living a productive life rather than isolating yourself.

If a relationship is over, honestly admit feeling the loss you suffered, do your grieving, and then accept that it is over and go on living. Recognize that this experience has taught you some vital lessons which can be used in the next relationship. See the highlights and go on. If you have loved before, you will love again. The confidence and inner strength you can draw from surviving will sustain you for further risks.

Other benefits to be gained from letting go of a relationship that wasn't meant to last are that as you continue to heal you will find your thinking sharpened, your judgment more reliable, and your concentration improved. As you become less self-preoccupied and reach out to others again, your feelings, responsiveness, and sensitivity become more alive. You will feel stronger and more independent. You have paid your way with tears, pain, and sadness but now you can smile again. You are stronger and more determined than ever.

Memories may return when you hear "your song" or catch a glimpse of him, but if you expect to feel sad again at these times, you know you aren't retreating into depression. You recognize the ebb and flow of healing and growing. You know it soon will pass.

Grace, like so many other women, knew she had to leave a bad marriage, but fear and inertia kept her hoping for improvements that never came. She finally made the break, leaving both husband and teenage children behind. "You know, asking my husband for a divorce was the really hard part," she said, shaking her head in wonder. "After that, finding a job, a place to live, and starting night school were all easy!"

Here is a plan to help you get through the pain of ending a relationship.

FIRST WEEK. Mourn, cry. Begin the healing process by admitting that you shared something deeply and now it is over. Be gentle with yourself. If you want to refuse social invitations, do so. Taking time to be alone and experience your feelings is necessary for recovery.

SECOND WEEK. Now that you are sure that the relationship is really over and there is no hope of patching it together again, get busy and "wash that man right outta your hair." Rip up old letters and souvenirs, use ink eraser to remove his name, address, and phone number from your address book. Tear up pictures and, if you feel dramatic, scatter the remains to the winds as a symbolic gesture. If you feel like communicating with him, write down everything in letter form. Pour out all the hurt and anger and sense of loss; tell him about the anticipations and the unfulfilled dreams. *Then burn the letter.*

THIRD WEEK. Change some of the interests you shared with him; stop going to that special restaurant or other rendezvous points. Start planning a new life without him. Buy a new wardrobe. Enroll in some classes, something exciting that you never considered before like belly dancing, wilderness survival training, pre-Columbian art, or auto mechanics. Learn a new musical instrument, give a party, take up a sport (racketball is great for relieving pent-up feelings), volunteer some time for charity, cultivate some new women friends, or begin some other absorbing project. Stay busy; don't worry at this point about being overly busy. Soon you will find you have made it through a full twenty-four hours without thinking of him.

FOURTH WEEK. Be aware of the ability to cope that you have used in the past weeks of change and adjustment. Feel the return of self-confidence and take stock of the good. You knew the joys of loving, you cared, you became involved. You learned to invest yourself. Think about what you have learned from the relationship and its ending. Think about the positive aspects you can draw on later. Remind yourself that there may be a far better relationship on the horizon that will flourish because of the self-knowledge and skills you have gained. Use your lovingness toward your family, friends, coworkers. Romantic love is only one form of loving. Rechannel your feelings and share them with others.

Now a well-deserved pat on the back is in order. You loved, you lost. But more important, you have won a new and richer life for yourself. Congratulations.

Risking Reaching for High or Higher Job or Offices. Until recently, few women sought top jobs in organizations or went after volunteer or elected office. Some had greatness thrust upon them; some, after their husband's death, inherited the position he held. Most, however, settled for what they were given. Today it's okay for women to openly challenge the establishments that put ceilings on their upward mobility, or shunt them off in dead-end slots. Ambitious women can come out of the closet and admit that, like their male colleagues, they too want in on the fast-track routes to higher position or office.

As more women enter the work force, as competition for top jobs gets even keener, moving nimbly from rung to rung—or even leaping two or three at a time—involves greater and greater risks. The Women's Movement has been about choice, primarily between a home, career, or combination of both. But one choice that is shrinking involves whether to work or not. More and more women are working because they have to, not because they choose to. Consider that one of three marriages now ends in divorce; consider that more women today are opting not to marry, or if married not to have children; consider that most women outlive most men by ten years; and finally, consider that women no longer work for five or ten years, but for twenty-five years or more.

What all these considerations add up to is that more women will seek careers rather than jobs, and careers almost demand upward progression and advancement. Even less ambitious women will be forced to raise their sights. Risking for promotions and higher pay, as well as risking campaigning for office, will become the order of the day and an accepted way of life.

You will have to forget the myth that the world of work is a fair place or that if you do your work well, rewards will automatically come your way. You will have to make plans and plan strategies; you will have to call on mentors and networks and all the support you can get. It's a jungle out there!

Obviously, risking for advancement requires all the skills we have discussed in other parts of this book. Going after that better job or office takes guts and, in some ways, a thicker skin that is required for other ventures. You can expect to be criticized and condemned. You can expect skirmishes and unfair attacks. A congresswoman told us she had even been subjected to bodily risks. Her life has been threatened and she has had bricks thrown through her windows. You risk your reputation, your current stronghold, your bankroll, and your friends.

But you can do it and it's worth it, according to most women who have taken these kinds of risks. Although some women report it's too lonely at the top to be comfortable and being a token at the top is even worse, and other women top out or quit because the rewards aren't worth it, the majority are happily ensconced in that upper echelon and love it.

"Talk about lonely at the top!" said Kay, a successful insurance agent in a large company. "I was not only lonely; some days I thought I was invisible because no one would talk to me."

For the first two years of her insurance career, Kay developed many friendships in the company. Both male and female colleagues went out of their way to be friendly and help her learn the ropes. "When I was a rookie in the business, I was no threat to anybody," Kay explains.

But that all changed when she got a promotion and decided to become serious about a career in the insurance business. She changed her hairdo and stopped socializing exclusively with women in the clerical ranks. She began competing for commissions and that's when the deep freeze began. Kay decided not to let the loneliness bother her.

She continued to compete toe to toe with her male counterparts and won an award for her sales volume. Now she finds she is slowly building respect and making new friends in the company, but mostly from people above her in the hierarchy.

"Men are less likely to accept women who stick their necks out and become serious about a career," says Kay. She is glad her husband is a very secure man.

When you select your target position, you can lessen the risk by careful planning and preparation. You can learn the rules of game and team playing. You can become more visible by giving above-and-beyond efforts to your present position that mark you as a comer.

Step back and study the big picture; learn to look at issues and priorities beyond your own unit or department. And by all means make it known that you're interested in moving up. If you're too shy to let your goals be known, you only confirm the stereotype that women aren't committed to careers.

Suppose your target is a vice presidency of your company. Do some research on how the current V.P.s got there. Did they move up out of sales or marketing or public relations? Chart the most likely path and get on it yourself.

Risking in the moving-up arena can be for the highest stakes. Go for it. Don't be one of those who cling to the sidelines.

Here are some steps to take to get you out there where the action is.

PROFESSIONAL SELF-ANALYSIS
AND CAREER PLANNING

Part I: *Barriers to Success*

Step One: Make a list of the barriers in your way. Answer the question: *What (or who) is preventing me from doing my job better and/or getting a promotion or better job?*
1.
2.
3.
4.

Step Two: Analyze the list and identify those items that are *inside the organization* you work for (IO) and those that are *inside you* (IM).

Step Three: Make a new list of all those aspects marked IO and break it into two subgroups, either *Can Help* or *Can't Help*.

Step Four: Do the same thing with the group marked IM—*Can Help* or *Can't Help*.

Step Five: Look again at the items in the two "Can't
Help" lists. If you are positive that you
can't do anything about them, cross them
out and forget them.

Step Six: Now concentrate on the "Can Help" lists
and decide on a plan of action. *What are
you going to do to try to remove or lessen
those barriers?*

Part II: *Skills Analysis (How Am I Doing?)*

The following are important skills that are needed to do
almost any job. Opposite each one, jot down a brief evaluation of how well you perform the skill. If you are not satisfied
with how well you perform the skill, also write out your action plan, or what you hope to do to improve.

SKILLS	EVALUATION	ACTION PLAN
1. *Planning and organizing* Examples: setting work goals, time deadlines, anticipating problems, taking responsibility, improving procedures		
2. *Communicating and interper-* *sonal effectiveness* Examples: listening and un- derstanding, resolving conflicts, selling ideas, con- ducting meetings and interviews, writing effective letters, reports		

SKILLS   EVALUATION   ACTION PLAN

3. *Supporting the boss*
   Examples: helping the supervisor gain support of others,
   adjusting to changing priorities, filling in for the boss
   without being asked

4. *Managing subordinates*
   Examples: motivating others
   to do better work, dealing
   with grievances, complaints,
   delegating, following through

5. *Handling specific situations*
   Examples: seeking feedback
   for self-improvement, maintaining balance between
   concern for work and concern
   for people, not jumping to
   conclusions

6. *Technical skills*
   Examples: keeping up to date
   on technical knowledge in
   field, efficiency in use of office machinery and
   equipment, skills such as bud-
   get making, accounting

7. *Other* (that are peculiar to
   your job or field)

Part III: *The Job Description*

Write a detailed job description for the job you hold. But
don't write down what *you* do, write the description for your

successor. Pretend you are leaving the position and you are preparing the job description for your supervisor to use in trying to find the best possible replacement for you.

Did any skills show up that you had not identified in the skills analysis?

Is there anything in the description that shows areas where you might do your present job better?

If you have a cooperative supervisor, have him or her also write a job description (before seeing yours) and then compare the two. Are there differences in perception, priorities, or anything else? If possible, discuss these differences at length and come to some mutual agreements.

Part IV: *Setting Goals*

Arrive at goals

Fantasize about the perfect job for you.

What kinds of work are pleasing, exciting?

What kind of atmosphere/business/organization would you most like to work in?

What are your principal strengths? What do you do best? What work do you most enjoy doing?

What do you have to offer your present employer or a prospective employer that he or she *needs*?

Do some further analysis and write a description of the job you feel you can do—either now or eventually. Design your own job and select the place you would most like to do it.

Part V: *Getting Training and Advice (Where to Go and What to Do)*

Talk to colleagues, boss, family.

Talk to people in the job or profession you have your eye on.

Check out training opportunities in your organization:

Are there defined career ladders?

If not, could you help get something started?

Check out training opportunities in professional associations.

Get counseling through personnel office or at the nearest college or university.

Take aptitude tests.

Read books, articles.

Take courses at night school.

Take an educational leave.

Take correspondence courses.

Investigate "University Without Walls" opportunities where credit is given for work and life experiences.

Attend workshops, seminars.

Map a personal development program—both long-range and in specific small steps.

Risking Starting or Changing a Career. If you're tired of a boring, traditional, or dead-end job or you're just starting out in or going back to the labor market, you have some different kinds of risks ahead. If you aren't sure what field to go into, get some counseling at women's centers in cities or on campuses. They can help you discover where your aptitudes and interests lie. What's more, they can tell you where the hot jobs are. No point in trying to break into a profession that is already overcrowded with overqualified applicants. And if there aren't many women in your chosen profession, so much the better. You'll be harder to overlook.

In larger organizations, there is a crucial difference between line jobs and staff jobs. Women have often been relegated to the staff positions, which are out of the mainstream: research assistant, personnel, librarian, administrative assistant. These can all be important positions but they are off to the side and not in the direct line of responsible decision makers who run the place. Staff people assist and advise; line people decide and determine. If you want to get on the fast track, aim at a line position, particularly one, like sales, that can be measured in dollars and cents.

In your shopping around for the right kind of employers, find out about their attitudes toward women employees and their affirmative action track record. Research their financial standing and their reputation in general. Large companies can provide you with more headroom, a greater variety of positions, and standardized job descriptions and pay scales. Smaller firms, on the other hand, offer more flexibility and may be more willing to let you prove yourself in nontraditional roles.

Resumé writing can be your best entrée or an employer turnoff, so don't just dash off any old thing. Keep it short, one page if possible. Present your accomplishments in a way that demonstrates how you will be able to produce results for the potential employer. Include your goals and the type of position you feel best suited for, as well as your principal work and educational history. To write an effective resumé, you must know what you have to sell as well as what the employer needs.

This is no time to be modest. Be sure to include the experience in supervision and organizing you learned as a homemaker or volunteer. Don't say "I helped," or "I participated" when it really was "I was responsible for . . ." If you aren't sure how to put a resumé together, get professional help. Even if you have to pay, it will be money well spent.

Few jobs are offered on the basis of a resumé alone. Send one when you know there is an opening or you have some in with the person doing the selecting. Write a brief cover letter that personalizes the information for each prospective employer and highlights why he or she should read the resumé. An excellent resumé may open the door for you, but it is the interview that clinches the job.

During the interview, bring up all your poise, confidence,

and communication skills. Make what you say focus on the job and the company by asking questions; don't just respond to what you are asked. And if you are asked discriminatory questions such as "Who will take care of your children?" or "Do you plan to start a family soon?" refuse to answer because a question asked of you that would not be asked of a male applicant is unfair and illegal. If you answer such a question willingly you have put yourself down.

Changing careers is no longer an unusual prospect because of the demand for new skills by new industries or organizations. Just look at what has happened to the electronic, computer, and video industries in recent years. So, although the risk right now may seem great, women had better start preparing themselves for future career changes, some of which may be forced upon them.

Career change can expand your experience and problem-solving ability. Moreover, you may not be aware of how transferable your talents are or how valuable they could be for the right employer. Instead of being frightening, a career shift can be both stimulating and rewarding.

Priscilla is one who made a successful career shift from being tops in one field to top of the heap in another. As a champion figure skater, Pris had contracts in professional ice shows thrust at her. But she and her husband had a dream they decided to follow. Selling everything they had, they drove to California and bought a run-down hotel in the desert. It was a lot of hard work, but today they own not one, but several famous health spas. In addition, they own a travel agency that specializes in health tours.

Was it worth it? Would she advise others to follow their dream vocation? "You bet!" Pris exclaims, nodding toward her eleven-year-old daughter, who is rapidly becoming a successful gymnast.

Yes, some changes of jobs or careers are not made voluntarily. What happens to you when your services "are no longer required"? Is it the end of the world or a blessing in disguise?

If this has happened to you, run, don't walk, to your bookstore or library for the book *Congratulations! You've Been Fired.**

Risking Changing a Lifestyle. Priscilla changed her lifestyle as well as her career, thus taking on a double risk. Women who go from high-powered positions to full-time motherhood, and vice versa, report the lifestyle shift takes a lot of getting used to. If the shift is consciously and freely chosen, the rewards are truly worth it. Lois is a case in point.

Back in the hills of Kentucky, Lois followed tradition and married at fourteen, having five children one right after the other. Fed up with farming, family producing, and cabin cleaning, she decided to make a break which she felt was her only chance to survive.

She packed her old pickup truck and a rented trailer with her children, her sewing machine, her piano, and a year's supply of bologna. Her supply of cash amounted to $200.

Lois liked the looks of Riverside, California, and decided to seek her fortune there. The first night of her new lifestyle found her and the children sleeping in paddle boats in a city park. Her first job in the "promised land" was cleaning toilets, but it paid enough for them to afford a small house. Lois and her eldest son both enrolled in junior high school and eventually went through high school together.

From that first little house, for which Lois paid $100 down, she went to better and better property and eventually became a real estate broker. Today she is an executive in the company for which she used to clean toilets. As one lawyer in Palm Desert confided, "I can't think of a single Board of Directors of any important organization around here of which Lois hasn't been a member, or is one now."

When most of us risk changing lifestyles, it may not be as

---

*Emily Koltnow and Lynne S. Dumas, *Congratulations! You've Been Fired. Sound Advice for Women Who've Been Terminated, Pink-Slipped, Downsized, or Otherwise Unemployed* (New York: Fawcett Columbine, 1990).

mind boggling as shifting from the hills of Kentucky to the sand of Palm Springs, but it can be just as important to us. Does our world lack color and life? Is our environment becoming ho-hum? Could be time to risk changing a lifestyle as well as a life.

Risking Starting or Buying a Business. How many women do you know who are self-employed or heads of their own businesses and decided to take that route because they were dissatisfied with working for other people and the way establishment organizations were run? We know quite a few and would have to include ourselves in that category. If you can't beat them, *don't* join them, but start out on your own, perhaps in a rival company, and do it better.

We've all heard about women who started small with an idea for a product or service and went up from there. Perhaps they worked out of their basements or garages and now have multimillion-dollar concerns, housed in their own high-rise buildngs. Maybe they figured out how to fill a need that they had felt—such as a day-care center, or a delivery van that takes health food lunches to employees, or a team of housewives who provide skilled and speedy housecleaning service. People in these kinds of business may not become millionaires, but they are happy being their own bosses and making money for themselves instead of for someone else.

Some small businesses fail because their founders thought only in terms of what they wanted to do with their time, energy, and talent and forgot to find out if there was a market for such a product or service. "Will people want to buy?" is a question that deserves hard study—not just a superficial look. Trying out your idea on a trial, part-time basis is a good way to find out and is a lot less traumatic than the bankruptcy court.

Working for yourself can be the hardest work you've ever done. To keep afloat, you may find yourself working seven days a week and even forgetting to give yourself a day off.

Self-employment requires such efforts and dedication and, at the same time, quite a bit of courage. Here are two examples of entrepreneurial risks from pioneer days.

At the height of the Gold Rush, Luzena Stanley Wilson and her husband left their prairie cabin with their two children, and headed west to California. While her husband rushed off to find gold, Luzena tried to think of a way to make some badly needed cash. She set up her cookstove and a table, bought provisions from the makeshift store, and by the time her husband came home that night there were twenty miners eating dinner, and another twenty waiting their turn. The business flourished and Luzena later took her husband into partnership.

In 1860, Bethenia Hill, daughter of an Oregon pioneer, found herself, at eighteen, the wife of a callous, bad-tempered husband and the mother of a frail child. She went against custom and advice and left her marriage. She survived not only a messy divorce trial but also the embarrassment of going back to primary school to get more education. She took in laundry and sewing, nursed the sick, working long hours to support herself and her child, In 1867, she opened a millinery business which did well enough to enable her to put her son through college, and she herself entered medical school at the age of thirty-eight.

Luzena's and Bethenia's stories are models of the process by which many new ventures come into being, out of need and near desperation, but backed by imagination and true grit.

A more modern example is Karen, who agonized over her desire to run a successful business, yet be of help to less fortunate people as well. "I owe my split personality to my parents," Karen explained. "I got my social consciousness from my mother and my business skills from my father. Thank goodness I found a way to live up to both."

Karen solved her dilemma by founding a company that invests in inner-city redevelopment projects. "I risked losing a lot of business friends who don't think social issues and business goals can co-exist. But I'm gradually proving them wrong."

Successful businesses often are started by people who are, for whatever reason, displaced from what might have been their life's normal path. Then, after the displacement, such people show a strong propensity to take control of their own lives and make something of them.

Seek out professional help when it comes to financing, accounting, capitalization, incorporating, advertising, and marketing. Other women in these fields would be good ones to hire and they, in turn, might become customers of yours. The library can give you lots of free help and you can also order many publications from the Government Printing Office either for free or at low cost. You could also write for *The Guide For Women Business Owners*, published by the U.S. Department of Commerce.

If you decide to buy an existing company or a business franchise, you should be prepared to invest time, money, and effort ahead of time researching all aspects. Here again, professional advice and assistance are the only way to go. Risking as an entrepreneur has enough potential pitfalls without trying to go it on your own.

Risking Going Back to School. Thanks to adult education programs and evening classes, this risk is not as great as it once was. You can test the water with a single course or workshop; you can get counseling from the sponsoring agency or college women's studies or career counseling departments.

Let's face and climb over those barriers that keep some women from picking up their education from whatever point it was interrupted.

1. *I don't know what I want to study.* See above. Get some advice. Talk to people. What interests you? What bugs you?

What is your goal? What do you have to learn in order to reach that goal?

2. *I don't remember how to study.* Rusty skills can be polished up again. Studying involves reading textbooks, listening to lectures and discussions, and then thinking about the concepts covered. A good technique is to try to anticipate what will be on the examination and practice writing out answers. Meet with the teacher and make sure you are grasping the important ideas she/he feels should be emphasized. Get together a group of fellow students and have regular study sessions. After a long absence from school, the first course will be the hardest. But each course after that will get easier and you'll soon be back in the swing of being a student.

3. *I don't want to compete with eighteen-year-olds.* Why not? So many older people are going back to school these days that they are no longer a novelty. This is particularly true for night classes and summer sessions. What's more, eighteen- and nineteen-year-olds can teach you a lot about how to "psych out" the teacher and what to expect. Make friends with them instead of thinking in terms of competition.

4. *What will my family and friends think?* Who cares? If they care about you they will be excited and pleased for you and they will try to be helpful. Nancy decided to go back to complete her college degree and, to her horror, found that she was scheduled into a class where her own son was enrolled. At first she tried to arrange a transfer but then had second thoughts. What really was the problem? What was she afraid of? It turned out to be a good learning situation for both of them. Mother learned a new appreciation for her son's intelligence and what it means to be a full-time student. Son gained some insights into his mother's goals and was proud of the way she could relate her experience to the theories discussed in class. P. S. They both aced the course.

5. *I'm too old to go back to school.* People have received

college degrees in their seventies and eighties. Age is immaterial when something you want to do is involved. A woman told her friend that she would really like to go back to school but it would have to be on a part-time basis which would take her ten years to get her degree and by then she would be fifty years old. Her friend very wisely asked, "How old will you be in ten years if you *don't* go back to school?

6. *I don't know if the money I put into education will pay off.* Now that's the toughest question of all. More education seldom hurt anyone and many people find sheer joy in learning itself, regardless of any practical application. If the job you're after requires a college degree or a Masters in Business Administration, then the answer is clear. But some business ventures or career opportunities are more available to people with experience in the field than to people with a lot of formal education. Situations vary. You'll have to be your own judge.

Are there any other barriers in your way? Are they reasons or excuses? We rest our case.

Which Are the Most Alien Risks for Men?

Although our attention has been focused on women and risking, along the way we interviewed several men. These bright, successful males all shared the belief that business risking is a piece of cake compared to the fear and vulnerability they felt when it came to interpersonal risks.

One of these men, George, who had been divorced for several years, told us that he had come to fear intimacy. "I feel I have to play it safe in personal matters," he said. "I don't even date any more because I don't want to lose my freedom or autonomy. Getting too close to a woman again would be too painful to risk."

Men today have had the traditional ground cut out from under them. They don't want to be burdened with the old stereotypes, yet learning new roles is agonizing and slow. When they played Prince to Cinderella, at least *they* were in charge. Now that the slipper doesn't fit, and women want to be managers of their own lives, the men may feel alone and unprepared.

As women practice their assertiveness and improve their own feelings of worth, they seek not only liberated males but androgynous relationships, where roles according to gender become unimportant. So far, it's a bridge over chancy waters, but let's hope for the day when women can risk more successfully in business and men lose their fear of risking intimacy.

You Can't Play It Safe and Risk, Too

You can't have it both ways. Fence-sitters are not risk-takers. Once you have decided that this is the risk you want to take and the time is right, you have no choice but to take decisive action. Once you have thought through all possible outcomes—both positive and negative—and carefully weighed your probabilities for success, then you focus on the factors you can affect and make them work for you.

Psychological defenses can be helpful in shielding you from potential harm. You can use them for second thoughts, to buy time to reconsider and decide on the best approach. A lifetime of defensiveness, however, can isolate you from both pain and joy. A rigidly defensive person who is completely safe, who never takes a chance, never really experiences life as it is. How can you be safe if you can't be real?

Remember the story of *The Velveteen Rabbit?* The rabbit was able to change to a real animal from a stuffed toy only after it had been loved so much that its shiny coat had gotten shabby and its button eyes were coming loose. You have to risk becoming a bit shopworn, too, if you truly want to be real.

Success doesn't always come to those who made good grades, had straight white teeth, or planned each day with the fever of a politician up for reelection. Success can also come to those who plan and work, as well as to those who seemingly stumble on opportunity and grab it.

One woman who could have played it safe but decided to risk was Jean who, at age twenty-five, was an office assistant for a large manufacturing concern. She was ambitious and wanted to move into management, so when an opening occurred for a foreman on the graveyard shift, she applied. Few women had ever been hired for the graveyard shift. Moreover, in the history of the company, no woman had ever been a factory foreman on any shift.

The personnel director tried to dissuade her by saying, "It's a dirty job with terrible hours. All the men on that shift are foul-mouthed and will probably harass you. Not only that, but some of the workers you would be supervising are old enough to be your father. How about waiting for some other job opening more suited to a young woman?"

Jean thought about her options for a few days. She wasn't thrilled by the hours, the job, or the men she would be supervising. The whole situation was very risky. But she also looked around the company at the scarce opportunities for people like her to break into management of any kind. She decided the foreman position represented a step up and future rewards outweighed any difficulties she would have with the workers and the loss of a normal social life caused by the shift hours. She pressed her application and was given the job.

Her male subordinates did give her a hard time, but she met each problem positively. She treated each whistle and attempted pass as a bid for attention, which she acknowledged with a smile and then asked about the man's wife or girl friend. She spent two years on the graveyard shift, gradually winning respect and increasing productivity as well.

Today Jean is a project engineer for the same company and is steadily moving up in the organization. As one of only six women in management, she has a high degree of visibility. As she says, she owes it all to the big risk she took in becoming foreman of the graveyard shift.

Risking Involves Some Loss of Control

Most people like the feeling of being on top of things, being in control. Yet unless the outcome is uncertain and you don't know just what it will be, then there's isn't a real risk; you're only going through the motions of a risk.

In business risks, there is no way you can make rigid, elaborate plans and expect to carry them out to the letter. Instead of control you need utmost flexibility to flow with what happens and make the best of all circumstances.

Business people who insist on tight control may be saying, in effect, that no one else is capable of managing as well as they do. These take-charge and hold-on-to-control types don't dare delegate anything but the scut work because it just might be revealed that someone else could handle the job as well or better than they.

Of course, the control issue is a major problem for parents. When do we trust our children to fly on their own? When do we stop protecting them from taking their own risks?

Monica is a mother who started teaching her children to take their own risks early. "You see it doesn't really matter if they win or lose," she explains. "Because my husband and I have encouraged all four of our children to take risks, they are open to so many more possibilities. We've tried to instill a risk-taking philosophy in them and they're all really open to life."

If someone offers you conditional love, which can be withdrawn at any time your behavior doesn't suit him, such love is being used to control you. Love used this way is cruel, no matter what form it takes or how sincere it appears when offered. To preserve this kind of love forces you to mortgage your self-esteem and self-respect. That's far too high a price for what you get. When you love someone else, you must give up all notions of controlling that person or the relationship. In order to be yourself and to have a real relationship, you must risk loss of control. But when you relax your hold on someone or something else, you experience a freedom and exhilaration that are the essence of liberation.

Some anonymous but very wise poet once wrote:

> If you love something, set it free.
> If it comes back to you, it's yours.
> If it doesn't, it never was.

You've Got to Have Heart

The cowardly lion is lovable and appealing but not an effective risk-taker. Stout heart and courage are essentials to risking. It might very well be painful and frightening to assume the responsibility for thinking and making choices, perhaps in a major way, for the first time. But fear is a matter of thought and belief that can be changed the same way it was acquired. A completely fearless person, of course, doesn't exist.

In Chapter One, we talked about some typical feminine fears that prevent successful risking—fear of disapproval, fear of failure, as well as fear of the unknown. These are real and persistent. Chances are they will never go away completely. The trick is to look fear in the eye, admit you're scared, and then go ahead anyway and do whatever it is.

If the risk you face is frightening, that's okay. The reason you feel afraid is not because you are weak but because you are real. The brave people are those who act in spite of fear, not those who have none. Only fools do not fear danger.

Think of your anxiety as nervous energy to keep you on your toes and functioning well. True, you're scared, but you're not scared stiff! You will not be immobilized or paralyzed by fear. You will not be ruled by fear but by a force that moves you through and beyond your fear. Remember the saying, "This, too, will pass." An additional comforting thought is to recognize that the other people involved in your risk are probably fearful, too. They, like you, have learned to hide their nervousness and get the job done.

When you are fearful, it often helps to think "What is the worst thing that could happen to me?" If you have been asked to give a speech to a large audience, and you believe you will have an attack of stagefright, what's the worst thing that could happen to you? You know from past experience that your hands may shake and rattle the paper, your knees may quiver and there may be cotton in your mouth. But the worst thing that could happen is that the audience will see you are a little uptight. They expect that. Even the most experienced speakers confess they are nervous when they first start speaking to a new audience. It's natural; it goes with the territory.

You may think that the worst thing that could happen to you in a public-speaking situation is forgetting what you want to say. Now that would be embarrassing. But the simple cure for that is to be adequately prepared with an outline of your main points in the order you want to make them. With notes in front of you, you can't forget.

When we face the fact that it is fear alone that is holding us back, then we can move ahead. Courage comes from instinct (even if only to survive), determination ("I'm going to make it through this.") and experience ("I've made it through before and I can do it again.").

Profiles of courage, success stories of women who risked and won, make good reading. Have books or articles like these handy when you start to feel shaky. Remind yourself about all those people who prevailed over what seemed like insurmountable odds and your risk will get back into better perspective.

Cynthia awakened in the emergency room of a hospital and realized her suicide attempt had failed. Anger welled up. She wanted to die. After twenty-four years of devoting herself to her husband and his career, she had found herself abandoned for another, younger woman. Her children were grown and gone. There was nothing to live for.

For several months Cynthia went from self-pity to despair and then one day decided enough was enough. If she couldn't succeed at dying, she might as well try living. She went back to school, took on some new interests and hobbies, and pulled herself up inch by inch to a new, satisfying life. Now she is grateful that she had the courage to live, and especially to live more fully.

How to Act Brave When You're Scared to Death

When we are afraid, we think the whole world knows it and that everyone is watching us. We feel conspicuous and somewhat like a bug on a pin under a microscope. But other people are really more concerned about themselves and their problems than they are about you and yours and probably aren't paying nearly as much attention to you as you thought. Every frog sees the world from his own puddle of water, often unaware of what's going on in the next puddle.

What this means is that the little signs that betray nervousness to you may not even be visible to other people. If you control your nerves to the best of your ability, put on a brave face (even if it's a big act), and go ahead with your plans, few people will even know that you were scared.

Since attitude change follows behavior change, if you act brave enough times, you will begin to feel brave. Before you know it, you are no longer acting. Courage becomes a part of your normal response. It may take time and it certainly takes effort, but courage can be acquired and developed. Try it.

What's Ahead for Risk-Takers in the '90s and Beyond?

The 90s are the decade of the woman entrepreneur. With competition at an all-time high and creativity and innovation dearly cherished, the corporate world desperately needs the risk-taker.

Consider Elaine Garzarelli, the market analyst who went out on a limb to predict the 1987 stock market crash and became a sought-after guru on Wall Street. What about Lynn Margolis, the University of Massachusetts researcher who proposed a ground-breaking theory of cell evolution and became a star among formerly hostile peers?

The world needs more women with psychological chutzpah. We need more great explorers and experimenters to break the rules, live on the edge, and kick out the stops of certainty and predictability. As more women enter the entrepreneurial arena, equal opportunity risking is surpassing the cultural mores of playing it safe that many of us have known. Welcoming change as a breath of fresh air in a stagnant traditional environment gives birth to new creativity and control over our personal and professional destiny.

Some researchers estimate that the changes that occur in the next twenty years will be comparable to what happened during the past hundred years. They are talking not only about the wide scope of change ahead, but also about the accelerated rate, which is predicted to be astonishing. As a result of so much change, the old security symbols will fade and true security will come from within the individual and from the quality of relationships and supports.

Lifespans will be longer. There will be food shortages but

people will have a better understanding of nutrition and how to get the most out of food supplements and vitamins. There will be totally new and as yet undiscovered sources of fuel and energy.

The world of work is predicted to change radically, too. Thanks to home computers and telecommunication, more people will be able to work at home, thus eliminating commuting to a separate workplace and its concomitant problems of too many cars, pollution, and high-priced gasoline. People will place less importance upon working for work's sake and fewer men and women will equate their personal worth with the value of their careers or professions. There will be more emphasis on being than on having.

So risk-takers will have new and different challenges. Planning and preparation will be even more important, but especially planning for future change. What seemed like a major risk yesterday may dwindle to insignificance tomorrow.

The next decades promise to be exciting and rewarding— for those who are ready. Will you be ready?

Summary

Embracing the alien, welcoming the unknown into your life gives risk-taking its excitement and zest. The most alien of risks for women are being hurt, admitting being hurt, entering new love relationships, ending unsatisfactory love relationships, reaching for high or higher jobs or offices, starting or changing careers, starting or buying a business, and going back to school. Successful risk-taking means that you can't play it safe and you can't keep tight control over all eventualities. Courage helps control fear and makes it possible to move through the fear to achieve your goal. Risk-taking will take on new dimensions and require different skills and approaches in the changing world ahead.

SIX

WORKING THROUGH CONFLICTS

AND CRISES

No one ever told you that taking risks would be easy or that all your trips will be smooth sailing. You know you should expect trouble. Although you won't be able to predict all the conflicts and crises you will encounter, experience points to some specific areas for which you should be prepared.

Attitude Is All

Whether you look at that rock in the path as a stumbling block or a stepping stone makes a whale of a difference. What does Old Man Trouble mean to you? An invitation to succeed no matter what, or stimulus to run and hide? Some people see problems, others challenges.

If you see more that is frightening than zestful in the risk you are about to take, you may still be reflecting early conditioning about what being a woman means and how women are supposed to behave. Old stereotypes die hard and slowly.

Women are experiencing rapid change and are trying their wings in a variety of ways. This new independence will be all to the good, eventually. But conflicts are still erupting because, unfortunately, our deeply ingrained beliefs are not changing as rapidly as our expectations and behavior. Many women and men still feel that men should be the boss. Many husbands are doing all the risking, including family financial decisions, out of habit and tradition regardless of talk about equality. Women without husbands or boyfriends are finding themselves unprepared to succeed in what has always been, and still is to a large extent, a male domain.

Although women are gaining ground, it's easy to be discouraged by the lack of economic gain. A recent headline in *The Wall Street Journal* read WOMEN MANAGERS GET PAID FAR LESS THAN MALES, DESPITE CAREER GAINS. On an average, women with the same education and experience as a male counterpart still earn less than 60 percent of the man's wage.

Progress has been made since the days when women were refused jobs or fired when a male applied because men were perceived as needing them more as family breadwinners. But deep down, this attitude is still with us. Women's place is still being defined by cultural norms and that place is still not side by side or toe to toe with high-achieving males. Equality and equal opportunity sound good but their reality is a long way off.

How should women feel about this? When the odds against making it in a man's world seem ridiculously high, women are tempted to become bitter and bitchy. Who can blame them? But on the whole, successful riskers must avoid discouragement and accentuate the positive. So progress is measured by molehills instead of mountains. Progress is progress, right? Consider the message contained in the Chinese character for the word "crisis." The symbols together spell both danger and opportunity.

Can You Handle Conflict?

Think back to your last experience with conflict. Perhaps it was an out-and-out battle with someone. Or maybe it was an uncomfortable feeling that all was not well between you and another person or a group of other people. How did you feel? How did you handle the situation? Can you figure out now in hindsight what caused the conflict?

Determining the source of conflict is not always easy because of unconscious or subconscious feelings, opinions, or values. A chance remark, now forgotten, by someone you admire could influence how you react to someone else. You may dislike Joe because he reminds you of your cousin Harry who gave you nothing but problems when you were kids.

Conflict exists on a continuum from a mild disagreement at one end to a shooting war on the other. Conflict occurs when there is a struggle for something, when somebody's motive is blocked by a barrier. Differences in values (proabortionists versus antiabortionists), scarcity (one job for fifteen applicants), and frustration from deprivation (burning a building may be the only way left to get the Establishment's attention) are among the many causes of conflict.

Most of us were taught to be nice little ladies and gentlemen and avoid conflict. "We can't talk about that, it's too controversial," is often heard, particularly in social situations. Nobody loves the person who argues about everything, but there is also no one more boring than the person who thinks everything is just wonderful. Then there is the self-appointed peacemaker who tries to smooth over every disagreement just when it is getting interesting.

Rather than avoid or smooth over conflict, we should welcome and encourage it. Conflict is the stimulus of thought; without it, life would be dull and unproductive. If we already agree about something, there is nothing left to talk about. What's the point of discussing "Two plus two equals four"? The discussion becomes useful only when someone says, "Wait a minute. I remember a time when two plus two equaled five." It's only when people share their different perceptions from different perspectives, acknowledging that these perceptions and perspectives clash, that problems can get solved. Walter Lippmann once said, "When everyone thinks alike, no one thinks much."

Conflict can occur inside you, when you are at war with yourself over a decision or the best course of action. Conflict, most generally, occurs between people, either singly or in groups, including groups as large as whole nations. For obvious reasons, let's focus on the interpersonal type of conflict.

When two or more people are in conflict, communication can be both a cause and a cure. Through communication we can define, express, and resolve differences. But how we try to get through to each other can also be part of the problem if we lack skill and sensitivity about what the messages mean to the other person. Research shows that too much communication can cause a disturbing message overload and can polarize antagonists instead of bringing them closer together. People need better communication, not necessarily more.

What is your style of managing conflict? Here are some sample situations.

1. A close friend has been the subject of unfair gossip and innuendo from people you both work with. She is being linked emotionally as well as professionally with her male mentor. Which of the following would you do: (a) wait and see what happens; (b) try to get everything out in the open so the problem can be resolved; (c) speak up for your friend, and explain away the rumors; or (d) go to the mentor and enlist his aid.

2. The executive committee of your club is arguing over which committees deserve to receive the most money and supplies. Which course would you take: (a) urge the group to make the split as fairly and evenly as possible; (b) tell the group to forget it, nothing is worth fighting over; (c) check the by-laws for guidance; (d) make sure people feel good and don't get angry even if that means your committee doesn't get as much as it deserves.

3. There are thirty-five hours of assistant time available for use between two offices you supervise. Each manager insists he needs thirty hours. Which way would you go: (a) listen to each manager justify his need and then make a decision based on that; (b) work with them to reach a solution acceptable to both; (c) consult district policy; (d) try to get each manager to settle for seventeen-and-a-half hours.

The options given for these three situations include five different ways of coping with conflict—*smoothing over* (1-c and 2-d); *compromise* (2-a and 3-d); use of *authority* (1-d, 2-c, 3-a and 3-c); *problem-solving* (1-b and 3-b); and *avoidance* (1-a and 2-b). All methods of coping have their time and place. If the boss and his or her spouse are arguing, avoidance would almost always be the better part of valor. But if you have established a pattern of avoiding conflict, you cannot move off dead center.

Problem solving seems to be the best method of dealing with conflict because the outcome is a plus for everyone, whereas compromise, although on the surface seeming the fairest of all solutions, can result in neither party being satisfied. Compromise has the connotation of forcing people to give up something and the reputation of creating only half-hearted commitments. Problem solving, on the other hand, is more of an adding to than a giving up, particularly when the decision is made by consensus.

A characteristic attitude toward conflict, however, is that resolution is possible only if one person or faction wins and the other loses. Games that end in ties are considered losses. It is true that some conflict must inevitably be cast in win/lose terms whether the winners are determined by force, arbitration, majority vote, or the toss of a coin. But a conflict settled this way won't go away because the differences that caused the conflict have not been eliminated. The best that can be said for a win/lose outcome is that a temporary settlement or an agreement to move ahead despite the conflict was reached.

A lose/lose outcome occurs when people refuse to acknowledge that conflict exists or they are unwilling to examine or discuss it. Sweeping it under the rug is only a temporary solution, in which everyone loses.

The ideal conflict resolution results in a win/win solution. Win/win works only if people are both willing and able to change, to zig and zag when needed, and are able to give other people the benefit of the doubt on the possibility that both sides in a dispute could be mistaken or correct. Everybody wins if the conflict solution gives them a solution they can live with and feel good about.

If the style of conflict resolution you usually use, that you are naturally disposed to, isn't working as well as you'd like, consider trying the other methods we have outlined. In addition, here are some specific techniques to add to your repertoire.

1. Look for and stress common ground. When you are in disagreement, you are apt to emphasize the points of difference and virtually forget that there are some aspects of the issue upon which both sides can agree. Recognizing that you are together on some points gives a foundation upon which you can build.

2. Compartmentalize the issues in conflict. Perhaps the problem is too complex for easy resolution. If so, break it into subpoints and tackle one at a time.

3. Insist that protagonists keep their arguments at the idea rather than the personality level. You will improve the climate and make conflict resolution possible if you say, in effect, to your opponent, "I don't like that idea you just expressed, but I like *you*."

4. Clarify goals and purposes. People in conflict are sometimes working at cross-purposes without knowing it. Make

certain that what you hope to accomplish is clearly understood and that you understand other people's goals.

5. Sleep on it. Sometimes when people have time to think back over a conflict, they can come up with solutions that previously eluded them. A cooling-off period, a temporary postponement, can be useful.

How Sharp Are Your Negotiating Skills?

Women are learning to negotiate as a means of getting what they want. They are learning the processes and strategies inherent in this method of resolving conflict. It has even been suggested that the marriage vows should now say, "Love, honor, and negotiate." Successful women negotiators "listen and synthesize the feelings and facts expressed to deal with both stated and unstated issues," says veteran negotiator Merrill Shields, a deputy Attorney General.

Not all conflicts are equally negotiable or even resolvable because so often "it all depends . . ." For instance, what's at stake? What kind of a relationship is it: casual, intimate, short-term, long-term? Who has the power? What is the context surrounding the conflict? What's going on at the surface and what is less obviously going on underneath?

Some people think they are negotiating when they say, "I want a 10 percent raise, or else." This kind of nonnegotiable demand is the opposite of negotiating. To negotiate, you need a range of options, not a fixed position. Flexibility is the name of the game. And don't forget negotiating goes on for other things besides money.

Take Jane who owns a motel. She wanted to go back to school and yet she felt so tied down to the day-and-night operation she didn't see how she could manage. Along came her answer in a man who offered to run the motel for her so she could be free at least part of the time to pursue her degree.

Jane went into the negotiation, feeling hopeless because she didn't believe she could afford the salary a full-time manager would demand. Yet the dialogue went something like this:

Jane: I really need someone to help me run the motel so I can go back to school. But I'm afraid I can't afford a full-time manager—and I know you have a family to support.

Tom: I would really like to help you run the motel and besides, I'm a good handyman who could also help you keep the place in good repair.

Jane: Just what I need, but . . .

Tom: Wait, let me tell you something you may not know. My real ambition is to become a writer and your motel office looks like a good place for me to write, when it's quiet, late at night, and we're waiting to fill the last vacancies. So how about me taking the night shift for you?

Jane: But I still don't think I can afford to pay you enough.

Tom: But don't you see, I'll be able to work for less because I can keep my other part-time job.

Jane: It sounds as if the money isn't that important to you.

Tom: Right! Having a quiet place to write is my biggest need right now.

Jane: And my biggest need is for free time. You're hired!

Now how's that for a win/win resolution?

Leverage is an important concept in negotiating. It's what you've got going for you at the time, your ace in the hole. When asking for a raise, you have leverage if you have another job offer or you've just done something great for your organization, such as saving it money. Women have not paid much attention to their leverage. Many, for instance, do not even keep a personnel file and throw away those priceless complimentary letters.

The process of negotiating is difficult to pin down because it varies with different contexts and different negotiators. Some women suspect it's a well-kept secret that only the power structure understands.

When you observe someone negotiating to buy a car or get a higher salary, you can easily see that each process is different and veteran negotiators recognize certain expectations on both sides. But inside an organization, each person must learn to spot the unwritten policies that the unsuspecting may trip over. "Oh, we don't do things that way around here," is a typical clue.

You'll have to learn for yourself how to find the most effective process to use in your particular situation. Watch how other people do it. Ask questions. This is where a mentor would be invaluable. (More about this in Chapter Seven.)

One last aspect of negotiating that women must pay more attention to is *preparation*.

Elizabeth thought she was prepared when she applied for a loan at her bank. She needed the money to keep her small business going and she had checked the current interest rate and figured she could swing the payments. But she was so woefully unprepared that she was in no position to negotiate; she had to take the deal the bank offered.

Let's backtrack and see what Elizabeth *might* have done to prepare. First, she could have checked at more than one bank and made a comparison between interest rates and loan terms, including requirements for collateral (security pledged to back up the loan). In addition, her cause could have been helped significantly if she knew the various banks' track record on loaning to women. Her comparison shopping would lead her to the best deal and give her a foundation from which to negotiate.

Finally, Elizabeth could have come out a winner if instead of going to her bank with just her company checkbook, she had prepared a packet of information to back up her application. Here are just some of the items her packet should have contained:

1. History of her company
2. Her personal financial statement
3. Company balance sheet
4. Company profit-and-loss statement
5. Accounts receivable
6. Accounts payable
7. Purpose of the loan
8. Source and terms of repayment

See what we mean about preparation? Skilled negotiators do their homework.

Do You Understand Power and Know How to Use It?

Power, like charisma, to which it is related, is difficult to pin down. It's easier to describe the results than describe the force that accomplished the results.

The word power means, literally, the ability to accomplish objectives, to move people. In other words, power is goal-directed.

Despite popular beliefs, power doesn't belong exclusively to the rich and famous. We all have potential for power but few of us recognize we have it or know how to use it. This seems especially true for women. Yet each of us not only has access to power, and the potential for more, but we also have the ability to empower others.

When we attempt to form an image of the intangible concept of power, it helps to think in terms of currencies. The most easily recognized currencies are, of course, power through *coercion* (military forces, the robber with a gun, the rapist with a knife); *physical strength*, which we often call "brute force"; and the real or imagined power associated with great wealth.

But there are many other power currencies that are less obvious. Here is only a partial list: intelligence, physical attractiveness, personality, knowledge, social status, political savvy, and communication skill.

Power doesn't automatically go along with titles or the delegation of authority. Many a newly promoted manager finds out that a title on the door doesn't necessarily increase her or his scope of control. The manager may, for example, have been given authority to make a decision on a particular issue but may or may not have the power to enforce that decision. True, there may be power in the position itself which is given (and can also be taken back) by those in higher authority. But if a leader also has the respect and commitment of subordinates, then that person also has personal power. The stars of the business and political worlds have both position and personal power.

Organizations are really power systems, where power is applied, resisted, and subjected to countervailing forces. Some of the power sources in the business world are obvious; some are so subtle that they are all but invisible to the outsider.

Dominance and Submissiveness. The next time you get a chance to watch two or more people in conversation, see if you can pick out the more dominant people. How will you do it? You can start by paying careful attention to who talks to whom and who talks the most. Dominant people initiate more topics and interrupt the flow of conversation more often; submissive people permit the interruptions without challenge.

Dominant people elicit personal information from others, without volunteering any of their own; they freely use other people's first names. Submissive people, on the other hand, give the impression of being unprepared and unsure and use disclaimers such as "I'm not really sure, but . . ."; they rarely use first names even when encouraged to do so.

Your analysis of dominant versus submissive people will need to take in many nonverbal characteristics such as the use of time. Submissive people allow other people to be in charge of their time.

Here are some additional clues to watch for:

	DOMINANT	SUBMISSIVE
Eyes	Looks away when the other person speaks	Watches speaker; looks away when eye contact made
Face	Impassive, poker face, no smile	Shows range of emotions, inappropriate smile
Posture	Relaxed, lots of movement	Tense, little movement
Movement	Large, expansive	Small, inhibited
Touch	Touches others	Yields to touch
Space	Expands, spreads out, invades others' space	Contracts, withdraws, yields to intrusion
Clothes	Comfortable	Constrained

Obviously, submissive people's behavior broadcasts impotence rather than power. Now that you've analyzed other people's projection of dominant or submissive qualities, what about your own? What messages do you send?

An interesting postscript to add to our discussion of the importance of understanding dominance in relation to power is the fact that dominance and submissiveness evoke their opposites. Hostility usually begets hostility in return. But submissiveness can actually bring out *more* dominance rather than less. Think about that one.

Many women communicate from weakness and inadvertently discount themselves because of their lack of vocal strength and projection. When you add to that the possibility that women are also telegraphing nonverbal messages of submissiveness, you begin to get a handle on the size of the problem. Irene Zarlingo, a national fundraiser for the arts and for the homeless, has raised millions as a volunteer. She is an undisputed leader in raising money for worthwhile causes. Her success is due to a positive attitude and a strong conviction that she will get what she wants. When she is going in to negotiate for a sizable donation, she starts by talking about many different subjects. She gets agreement by interjecting questions that require an affirmative answer: "Don't you think so?" "Yes" becomes a natural response. If conversation falters, and someone says "well," she replies, "well what?"

Pay attention to the sounds made by successful, powerful people. Their voices are apt to be forceful, clear, unhesitating, and in the lower rather than the higher ranges. Vocal qualities can be changed. If you are unhappy with your voice because it doesn't carry to the back of the room, because it sounds tentative rather than firm or because it squeaks when you get nervous, do something about it! Fast!

One thing you can do is work to lower your vocal tone. Your voice can be lowered just as you reach for a lower note when you are singing. Get in the habit of listening to yourself and reaching for a lower note. If that process isn't sufficient, consult a professional voice coach or speech therapist. A voice that says what you want it to—both verbally and nonverbally—is worth working for and is attainable.

Women and Power. If you consider the fact that women have not as a rule sought power for themselves and the fact that male chauvinism has deliberately prevented women from achieving any real power, you come to the conclusion that women are really powerless.

If this condition is ever to change, women must take another look at what power is and does, recognize its usefulness, and rid themselves of all those negative connotations. Power is not evil in itself; power just is. As women, we need to defuse the emotional charge in the concept of power and learn to claim ownership of our own personal power potential.

Whether she recognizes it or not, a woman has had to deal with power issues at home and in the family. This is where she learned her style of exerting and/or resisting power, along with the development of her own attitudes and values. Think about these important family power issues: food, love, independence, recognition, friends, respect, protection, sexuality. And what about those powerful issues involved in separation or divorce negotiations: interdependence, money, displacement, child custody, marketable skills, survival?

Although it may be subconscious on their part, most men perceive women as having little or no power. Even those few women who appear to have made it in the man's world of business and high finance have to work harder than men to be listened to and taken seriously. Unless they recognize the powerless position they have been given, unless they assert themselves and deliberately grab for some of the power, they are in a no-win game.

One of the saleswomen we interviewed said, "I sometimes go to a potential client with a male colleague as a partner. If the two of us are trying to sell another male, I find myself left out while the two of them talk. They quickly establish a bond from which I am obviously excluded. But I won't let them get away with that any more. When I see it happening, I move my chair so they cannot ignore me and I jump into the conversation and insert my viewpoint. I try to say something very technical or detailed to prove my right to be there as an equal."

Another woman we talked with, however, has not yet been able to resolve her problem with the male attitude. She said, "I try to help my father with his business problems but he ignores me. If my husband tells him the same thing, he listens. My father has had a hard time thinking of his daughter as a successful businesswoman."

Indirect Power and the Power of No Power. People with little or no power (and who feel that they have no hope of acquiring real power) learn to manipulate others in order to get their way. Rather than saying straight out what they want, what they think and feel, they use devious, indirect means. They use a form of power without confrontation, while maintaining apparent innocence about what they are up to. Take the child who plays his parents against each other ("But Daddy said I could!") or the wife who has a way of burning the toast on given occasions or who "accidentally" starches her husband's underwear.

Some people who appear to be submissive and the helpless victim in a power struggle, may, in fact, hold a form of tyranny over those with the real power. The burden is placed on the powerful to take care of the weak. "You wouldn't kick me when I'm down, would you?"

As an example, there is a management training game in which two people are paired off and asked to decide which of the twosome is the "Top Dog" and which is the "Bottom Dog." The person designated as Top Dog is then given the assignment to try to persuade the Bottom Dog to change in some way—in thinking, feeling, or behavior. The common but mistaken assumption is that the Top Dog has the power in such a situation. In fact, all the Bottom Dog has to do to win is *nothing!* By being noncooperative and nonresponsive, the Bottom Dog defeats the Top Dog and comes out on top.

We are not recommending either the indirect or the passive approach to power. Instead, we are urging women to be open and honest about their use of power. First, they must recognize that they *do* have power, perhaps not as much as they would like, but it's there. Next, they must learn to fully utilize that power instead of giving it away to others. We believe that the best power posture for anyone to have is the feeling of being empowered from within, along with the knowledge that you have resources which other people need and want.

We have too often confused influence with power. Many of us enjoy the influence associated with working in local political campaigns, but women have failed to organize sufficiently to elect people regionally and nationally.

We also lack economic power, despite the fact that women now own 43 percent of the country's registered stock. Yet owning stock is more than receiving dividends. Women will have true economic power only when they work to get on boards of directors and when they ask hard questions of the companies in which they own stock.

Now that women are exerting some economic muscle in earning their own living, in acquiring and using credit in their own names, they are developing power over their own destinies. Independence, both economically and psychologically, is the key connection between money and power.

How Can You Get More Power? Among the ways that women can gain more power are the following:

1. *Through learning.* Reading this book is a start. Reading other books, taking classes, going to workshops, and interviewing powerful people are all good ways to educate yourself.

2. *Through performance.* After you have successfully used

your own power to get what you want—even in small ways—your reputation will begin to build. What's more, your success will give you greater self-confidence in the next encounter and you will begin to look and act more powerfully.

3. *Through ability to get results.* Along with your growing reputation, you will be helped by people being aware that you know how to get things done. Power comes from knowing the right buttons to push and how to move things along in the direction you want them to go.

4. *Through expertise.* If you are an acknowledged expert in your area, and if you consistently demonstrate your experience and knowledge, you will invariably have more power.

5. *Through credibility.* If you continue to prove that you do your homework, and know what you're talking about, you have unquestioned competence, and you expect to win, you will develop high credibility. Your poise, objectivity, and the positive way in which you communicate also contribute to the establishment of credibility.

6. *Through allies and connections.* This is power by association. You may know people in high places or be affiliated with a powerful organization or institution, and thus are able to use these connections to augment your own power.

7. *By acting powerfully.* When we square our shoulders and move ahead as if we have all the power we need, power has a way of finding us. Unless a woman risks testing her power, she does not find a sense of personal security and is never sure of her strength. What is the result? She spends the rest of her life testing her defenses instead.

Cover Your Assets

We have talked about the connection between money and power, but more needs to be said about the relationship between women and their unmighty dollar. How many successful businesswomen do you know who have turned over the management of their money to men? Instead of dealing with their fear of money, learning how to save and spend with skill, they rely on their husbands, their bankers, their lawyers, their brokers, or good old Uncle Charley. Even when the male power figure they depend on has their best interests at heart, they have, in effect, put themselves into financial bondage.

Carol Ann Wilson, financial planner and co-author of *The Survival Manual for Women in Divorce,** says that women fear handling money and if they get up their courage to invest, they continue to invest conservatively. What the fear is about, according to Wilson, is that they will become homeless bag ladies. This fear may not be groundless when you consider that after a divorce, the average woman's income decreases by 73%, whereas the man's *increases* by 43%.

If you feel victimized or manipulated by money, if you engage in compulsive spending and the "Shop Til You Drop" habit, you need to change your ways and attitudes and fast. Make a decision to learn how to handle money wisely and profitably. Accept responsibility for your own financial present and future. If you make these changes, you will feel more confident and truly empowered. And only then will you be capable of successful financial risk-taking.

Do You Manage Time Well?

Many people keep talking about all the great things they will do whenever they get the time, forgetting that they already have all the time there is. We've been allotted the same number of hours in the day and days in the week; the difference is in what we do with that precious commodity, time.

No matter how busy you feel you are, you do have spare time—perhaps measured in minutes rather than hours—but

*Carol Ann Wilson, *The Survival Manual for Women in Divorce* (Boulder, Colo.: Quantum Press, 1990).

time nonetheless at your disposal. Time management calls for planning, discipline, and energy.

If time gets away from you, with little to show for it, then try to follow all or most of the following ideas, even if it means you must try to change some lifetime habits. Most experts in the management of time agree that the following aspects are the most important. These suggestions work.

1. Develop a game plan. Start each day working toward your goals. Write out a "To Do" list and check it for progress at the end of the day. Lists are the key to good organization.

2. Arrange your "To Do" list in categories, such as A for requiring immediate action, B for the most important, C for lower priority, D for items that are pending and will have to wait a while, and E for material you must read. No matter how tempting the lower priority items are, start working on the As and Bs until they are done.

3. Don't procrastinate. Get working as soon as you can without waiting for that big block of time that keeps eluding you. If you're frittering away time on unimportant things (rest and relaxation are *not* unimportant) you're engaging in escapism and robbing yourself of your most precious asset.

4. Avoid clutter. Don't be put off by distracting piles of paper. Try to handle a piece of paper only once instead of moving it around on your desk.

5. Delegate as much as possible, not only to your subordinates at work but also to your children at home.

6. Take breaks. Avoid decreased energy and consequent boredom by resting regularly and moving around frequently. Get up and away from your work at least once every hour. Your concentration and efficiency will be improved if you don't try to keep at it too long at a stretch.

7. Give yourself permission not to be perfect. Striving for perfectionism is a waste of time.

8. Don't be afraid to say no. Be tactful but firm when

anything or anyone tries to get in the way of your priorities.

Can You Handle Both Success and Failure?

We have already said that a fear of failure might be masking a fear of success. When you plan a big risk, you'd better be really sure you want what you're after because that is exactly what you're going to get.

For example, you decide to risk starting your own business. What if the business succeeds even beyond your dreams? Will you be equipped to handle the pressures of adding staff and managing people, increasing work loads and responsibilities, finding adequate space and planning for expanded marketing and on and on? Best that you think through the total price of success before you risk. Successful risking often turns up more than roses.

Once you, the successful risk-taker, make progress in your career, personal development, or attainment of your goals, you may find yourself in the company of saboteurs. Colleagues, family, friends, and even casual acquaintances are all candidates for the friendly enemy list.

How will you know if you are being sabotaged? See if any of the following situations sounds familiar.

1. You are rushing to meet an important client and your child chooses that moment to stage a temper tantrum.

2. You attempt to describe a business problem to your husband or boyfriend and he comments on how unfeminine you are beginning to sound.

3. A story appears about you in the paper and a friend you previously thought was well meaning, calls to ask how much you paid the writer.

4. You have been selected to receive an important award

and none of your friends or family has time to accompany you to the ceremony.

5. A special delivery letter arrives for you and the family member who was home at the time forgets to tell you about it for several days.

Sure, all of these events could be accidental as well as purposeful. It just seems human nature, unfortunately, to try to take away from someone's achievements, even subconsciously or inadvertently.

Although we don't necessarily belong to the "grin and bear it" school, sometimes that's the only way to handle saboteurs because if you confront them, the problem is accelerated and may even be escalated out of proportion.

It may sound like an out-and-out contradiction, but for many women failure is easier to cope with than success. For one thing, they have had more experience with failure and know more what to expect.

But despite loneliness at the top, despite the hassles and the lurking saboteurs, most of us will opt for success every time. Bring on the success, we'll gladly pay the price.

Take Only Your Own Risks

Be sure that it's your own risk you're taking and not someone else's. Women have a tendency to try to fulfill someone else's dream. Say a friend has an idea for a project and doesn't want to take the risk himself so he talks you into it. You may agree and take the plunge but since you have neither the interest nor the faith in the project that he does, the risking odds will be against you. In that situation it would be far better for you to urge him to take his own risk, with help from you, rather than your going out on a limb on behalf of someone else's project.

Similarly, it's bad policy for you to try to get others to take risks that are rightfully yours. A mother who never was able to realize her special dream may encourage a daughter in that direction so that she can vicariously live through the experience.

Until we each assume responsibility for our own life goals and their consequent risks, we cannot find happiness or achievement by either taking on someone else's risk or by letting Georgia do it for us. Effective risking requires the clear direction and commitment that can come only from charting our own course and steering our own ship.

Summary

Most risking byways are strewn with conflicts and crises. People who risk successfully are apt to think in terms of challenges rather than problems. Conflict is both inevitable and beneficial and the key is to learn to use it productively instead of running away from it. Understanding and using power is a neglected aspect of most women's education, and the better you manage your time, the better risk-taker you are. One potential crisis comes, oddly enough, in the shape of success, and another can occur if you either take someone else's risk or try to get someone else to take on yours.

SEVEN

YOU ARE NOT ALONE

Risking, like other creative activities, can be a lonely business. Self-discipline must be coupled with private time alone to think and plan and create. But too many women have felt that they *must* go it alone because others wouldn't understand or because it was somehow cheating to depend on help from other people.

To some, it may be a blow to the ego to have to admit they need help. To these unfortunate people, having to recognize their dependence is bad enough, but when they actually have to ask for help they feel demeaned and diminished.

Consider the young woman who was trying to juggle a full-time job, take care of a house, husband, and child, and also pursue a graduate degree. Deep down, she was angry that her husband was not handling more of the household and child-care responsibilities, but she never acknowledged the anger and let the situation go on and on. Even when the inner rage was transformed into migraine headaches, the problem was still not resolved. When asked by a friend why she didn't *ask* her husband for more help, she replied, "But he ought to be able to *see* I need more help—he ought to *know!*"

This woman typifies those who have not asked for what they wanted or needed on the false assumption that the boss or the husband or the child is a mind reader who ought to know how hard they work and exactly what their needs are. It

153

can come as a surprise to learn that the folks who people our world are neither mind readers nor philanthropic. The answer, of course, is to set our goals and, if we discover that we can't reach them on our own, to look at all the sources of aid around us and go for the help we need.

What Kind of Support Do You Need?

Perhaps all you need is a warm hand to hold or your full daily quota of hugs and warm fuzzies. Ask yourself who really cares about you? Who encourages you to dream your own dreams and be more fully who you are? Who stands by you unconditionally when others question the sanity of the risk you are about to take?

Or perhaps all you need at this point is a good, active listener who hears you out without forcing in his or her ideas, opinions, or suggestions. Good listeners, who are nonjudgmental and ask helpful questions (rather than make assertions or give advice) are rare.

In addition to these kinds of *emotional* support, you may need *psychological* help which can come from knowing that certain people are in your corner, that you have your own rooting section cheering you on. It also helps to know that other women have risked in the way you are contemplating and that they won. *Financial* help could also be one of your needs and most of us have discovered that banks are not the only sources of money. Maybe you could use some *technical* support. Is there someone in your organization or elsewhere who can supply you with answers, or data, or advice that will tip the risking odds more in your favor?

Some Ways to Build Support

Here are some steps and thought starters to get you going. *Step One:* Continue (harder, if necessary) getting to know who you are as a person. (Go back and skim Chapter Two again for suggestions you haven't yet tried.)

Step Two: Trust yourself to know what's best for you. Cast out lingering doubts and mental put-downs.

Step Three: Open up to more friendly associations with others. This means getting yourself out and among people. It also means that you initiate contacts and stop sitting back waiting to be chosen.

Step Four: Decide what you want to do and the kinds of help you'll need in order to do it well and quickly.

Step Five: Build a community to support your efforts. Surround yourself with people who validate your existence and make you feel good about yourself and life in general. Make sure they are energy givers, not energy depleters, as we pointed out in Chapter Four.

Here's another suggestion. Pretend you are having a gala party to celebrate life and all the good things that have happened to you. You want to surround yourself with joyous, fun-loving people. Whom would you invite?

Or how about this? Make a list of twenty friends or acquaintances and list the contribution each makes to your life. Now look over the same list and write down the contribution you make to each of their lives. What do those lists tell you?

Support and Comfort Can Come From Many Sources

Anyone or anything is potentially the beginning of a support system. Multisources of aid can be found if we look, listen, ask, reach out, and engage in dialogue.

A natural starting point is your family. We sometimes take family support for granted and fail to work at being a truly mutually supportive group. Support is a two-way stretch that calls for both giving and receiving help. If families are accustomed to rallying around and to keeping communication open and authentic, the home front can be the prime booster and bolster of your confidence.

Family systems are complex and the degree of closeness between individuals can vary greatly. Virginia Satir describes the bond as a rope which is attached to all family members. Some stretches of rope are taut and others loose, but disturb the rope between two people and you disturb all.

Single-parent families offer a particular challenge to building supports. Often a newly divorced or widowed parent tries to play superman or superwoman and be everything to everyone. After that unrealistic phase passes, and any leftover feelings of guilt or self-pity are thrown out, it's time to get down to the business of organizing support. Family powwows to outline household chores and areas of responsibility can be invaluable. Even small children can handle such assignments as making their beds, taking out the trash, and loading the dishwasher. Older children can plan menus, shop, cook, and be responsible for their own laundry. Even though they may grumble, children gain maturity and a sense of accomplishment from shared work and doing their part on the team.

Risking under these conditions often involves erratic schedules, unprepared or uneaten meals, and creative communication centers. Messages on the refrigerator, or the bathroom mirror, or on the dog's collar, as well as fresh dandelions in a jelly jar are all attempts to keep the lines and the caring clear.

Extended families, both in the older sense of including grandparents and aunts and uncles and cousins, and the newer meaning of selecting close friends to be a part of your extended family, are additional sources of support. Today's nontraditional family encompasses people with similar goals and values who share resources and decisions, and who develop commitments to each other—whether or not there are legal, blood, adoption, or other ties. Despite time and distance, such extended family members usually come through to shield, lift up, or sustain you when you need it most. But the bonds of commitment have to be carefully built and regularly nurtured and maintained.

Love relationships, live-in style or otherwise, can be a woman's major support. Today's woman, however, enjoys a far greater range of choice, including the choice *not* to have a love relationship. Thoroughly modern Millie is able to transcend old stereotypes and dictated roles. Even if her lover is on her staff, she can say, "I love you, Roger, but you're fired!" As tough as she wants to be in the boardroom, the modern woman can be tough or gentle or both in the bedroom. Whether she chooses a younger man (because those her own age are either unavailable or threatened by her) or an older man (because she loves him, not because she wants another daddy) or a blue-collar worker or someone of a different religion or nationality or ethnic background, the important point is that she has choices.

The *neighborhood* offers another source of assistance. Futurists say that the isolation and alienation caused by six-foot privacy fences between neighbors will give way to more closeness and sharing. For economic as well as emotional and spiritual reasons, there will have to be more bonding in the future. What support can you give to and get from your neighbors? For a start, agreeing to keep an eye on each other's property allows you to go away with less fear of being robbed. Bringing in each other's mail and papers, accepting packages, and reciprocal baby-sitting are only some of many possibilities.

Sometimes called the best thing that ever happened to people, *friends* can also offer tremendously helpful support and assistance. Remember the old saying that you're stuck with your relatives but you can choose your friends. Friends have more potential to fill the needs you have for emotional nourishment than even the family does. With friends there is no preset idea about how you have to relate; there are fewer demands and more acceptance.

Here are some ways to evaluate the friendships in your life right now.

1. Imagine you have just inherited a magnificent estate along the Côte d'Azur that is isolated from human contact. No one is there but you and the friend or friends you have invited. With whom will you choose to share your hideaway? Why?

2. Suppose you have been falsely accused of shoplifting in a department store and have been taken to police headquarters. You are embarrassed, shaken, and scared. You are allowed one phone call besides the one to your lawyer. Whom would you call? Why?

People who have similar goals or interests, but with whom you do not have emotional linkage, are allies. Colleagues and allies can be terrific aids. One woman deliberately cultivated the friendship of two men who had jobs similar to hers but were in a different department. By seeking them out, buying them coffee or lunch, she gradually developed two important allies. When a project she was working on got shot down or when her ideas were ignored in a staff meeting, she could ask for advice and counsel. Because the men were neither close colleagues or competitors of hers, they could freely say, "Well, here's what you did wrong. Next time, try this."

Clubs, associations, and *professional groups* are other sources of support and learning. Write down a list of all your interests, both professional and personal. Then check the Yellow Pages and meeting notices in the newspaper for groups that you could join. If existing groups don't seem appropriate, consider forming your own. Also, don't forget adult education classes and workshops as additional sources of ideas, education, and friends.

Your work and home *environment* can provide needed support. In Chapter Four we discussed how an appropriate environment, organized the way you want it and need it, can give you energy. Such simple things as pencils and paper by the phone and calendars for better time management can give you vital backup when you are preparing to risk.

Finding a Mentor

Most successful men and women report that a key factor for them on the way up the corporate ladder, or in the process of starting their own business, was that they were privileged to have one or more mentors. Their mentor, usually someone older and usually male, was someone who took an interest in their career and development, who helped open doors and who either pushed or pulled them along.

Unless their fathers were their mentors, women have not found it as easy as men to be taken on as someone's protégée. And finding a successful woman role model to emulate has been extremely difficult because there just aren't that many around. Another discouraging factor has been that male mentors have too often taken more than a professional interest in the female under their wing. With sexual favors in mind, the mentor puts the woman in the double bind. She needs his help and she may be truly fond of him, but she also knows that sex and business are a bad mix and lying down is not the way to climb a ladder.

Unfortunately, businesswomen have always been subjected to sexual harassment, unwanted passes, or insulting innuendo. And even when she skillfully sidesteps these obvious traps, a woman can find her career in jeopardy because of malicious gossip. These no-win situations almost always find the woman having to move out while the male remains protected by his network. So proceed with caution when choosing a male mentor.

Career women who haven't had a mentor have been developmentally handicapped, perhaps without knowing it. The fortunate few with mentors say their careers really gathered momentum when a mentor helped them grow by offering suggestions and constructive criticism. What's more, the mentor acted as a buffer between them and clients or colleagues who felt threatened by able women.

Mentors can make all the difference. It has long been an accepted fact that young people, in professions and in general, learn better by studying with an older and wiser veteran. Some corporations today are beginning to experiment with formalizing this practice and making it company policy. The Jewel Companies of Chicago, for example, assign a corporate sponsor to each new employee. If this kind of procedure catches on, it will be a tremendous boost to women. If the buddy system is deliberately rather than spontaneously arranged and everyone has a sponsor, women with male mentors should be less frequently singled out as targets for resentment and whisper campaigns.

If you have a mentor, risk-taking can be attempted with more certainty and less chance of failure. Your mentor can not only give you opportunities to try the high wire but also hold a net below to break your possible fall.

Look around at the successful people you admire. What is it that attracts you to them? What qualities would be of greatest assistance to you? The helper/helpee relationship usually develops through mutual admiration, through shared values, interests, and ambitions. The young person needs guidance and advice; the older person has been there and can point the way. If you don't have a mentor, give thought to finding and developing one. On the other hand, if there is no Mr. Right on your horizon, don't waste time pining for one. Get on with it.

Being a Mentor

Women who have made it have a responsibility to be a mentor to younger, less experienced women. The Queen Bee who sits in her high office, believing that because she made it in a man's world, other women ought to be able to make it, too, is selfish and shortsighted.

Successful, fast-track executives make a point of training their own successors. Helping another woman move up behind you as you move up is not only helping women everywhere, it's good business. Mentoring, of course, has risks as well as rewards. One risk is that your mentee might outdistance you and/or become an ungrateful, disloyal competitor.

A true leader is known by the people she develops, not by those she dominates or rises above. Helping others inevitably means you help yourself. You can never repay your mentor for the help you got, but you can pass along some of the know-how and support to others. And one way to do this is through networking.

Networking

Fortunately, with the advent of new awareness and the raising of feminine consciousness, women are recognizing the necessity of banding together for the formation of mutual support groups. Networks that do for women what the familiar "Old Boys' Network" has done for men, are springing up in many different forms all over the country. Networks have been called the feminist phenomenon of the 1980s. To keep track of the burgeoning movement, there is even a network of networks!

Women are learning the process of advancing themselves and each other through the established business, or political, or social order. When you realize that U. S. Labor Department statistics show 48 percent of all jobs come through personal contacts, you are not surprised to see women forming all kinds of new and effective buddy systems.

Although she may not be your favorite person, a woman who is higher up in your organization needs and deserves your support. Giving the higher-up whatever encouragement or help she needs benefits both of you because if women at lower levels don't support women at higher levels and they fail, it will be three times harder for the next woman to make it.

Despite women's advances in the business world, we still hear about woman to woman sabotage. In her book, *Woman To Woman: From Sabotage To Support*,* Judith Briles says women need to confront the saboteur (sabotesse?) instead of merely hoping the behavior will stop on its own. Unless they confront the person, women being sabotaged are giving out the message that it's okay to hurt them.

Since all nonproductive or destructive behavior has a cause, another solution is to try to figure out what is behind the dirty deeds. Does the individual have some unmet needs? One woman in the advertising department of a large manufacturer was given the assignment of organizing and writing the company's first inhouse newsletter. At every turn, she found herself blocked and discovered that all the problems stemmed from one woman, a long-time employee. The editor asked to interview the troublemaker and featured her with a picture on the front page of the first issue. To no one's surprise, the sabotaging stopped. A little recognition goes a long way.

Business and professional networks help women make business contacts, learn about career advancement opportunities, find suitable women for job openings, and meet po-

*Judith Briles, *Woman To Woman: From Sabotage To Support* (Chico, Calif.: New Horizon Press, 1987.)

tential clients. Networks for women are booming because they work.

Women's networks, however, are in danger of being weakened or even scuttled by some women who are joining them only for their own selfish needs. In *Executive Female* magazine, Mary Scott Welch wrote:

> . . . certain newcomers to networking are missing the sustaining, I might say inspiring point of it all: networking is a *mutual* support system, not a gimme-gimme gimmick. They don't seem to understand that you have to *offer* help at least as often as you *ask* for it; you have to put in as much as you take out of the pool of women helping women.*

Being a Team Player

You hear a lot these days about the importance of teams and team playing in business. You also hear and read that women do not make good corporate managers because little girls have not learned how to be team players as boys have.

How do women overcome this lack of experience? First, they have to recognize the great importance placed on teams in business and the professions. Next, they have to identify the teams of which they are already members and try to find ways to be a better team player. This means developing more group-mindedness and the we're-all-in-this-together feeling.

One woman, with the help of her husband, recognized that she had been self-centered rather than team-centered when she had applied for a higher position in her company. When she got a "Don't call us, we'll call you" type of answer, she went home, bitterly disappointed, and poured out her frustrations. "Hold on, there!" her husband said. "Why are you getting so worked up? Why are you taking this so personally? You don't have all the cards and yet you're acting

---

* Mary Scott Welch, "Keeping in Touch," *Executive Female* (May/June, 1980), p. 54.

as if you do." Reluctantly, she decided her husband was right. She had been on an ego trip instead of thinking in terms of what was best for the company.

Another professional woman explained how she was able to make the transition to team playing. "My mother taught me to be nice and if I didn't like someone not to play with that person. But in business, you *have* to play even if you hate the other person's guts. You have to put team playing first and ignore personality clashes."

Who Is Always Your Best Friend and Ultimate Support? You!

Making effective use of support from others can come only after you have decided that you are worthwhile and deserve support. Are you your own best friend? Do you encourage yourself to be self-actualized and the best you can possibly be?

Believing in yourself and looking out for Number One, without guilt or embarrassment, are vital parts of self-support. Your self-esteem must be high and positive and you must be willing to take responsibility for your own life. You must shed the skin labeled "victim" and acknowledge that directly or indirectly your choices have caused whatever has happened to you.

You must have or develop an unconditional acceptance of yourself. Despite mistakes, defeats, and failures, you still consider yourself to be an innately worthy and important being. Unfortunately, many women have stored up a reservoir of negative emotional reactions, causing them to feel dependent and inferior. Low self-esteem is evidenced by the woman who has not exercised her assertive muscles and made the mental statement, "I am *me* and damned proud of it."

Everyone sooner or later comes to a time when the chips are down and she is forced to stand alone. If you are not conditioned to supporting yourself, you could easily falter under other people's objections.

Answer the following questions and carefully analyze the results:

What do I do to sabotage my own success in building support?

What traits do I have that impede me from being my own best friend?

What are the situations that undermine my own self-confidence?

Do I have more support at home or work? Why?

Am I as fully supportive of others as I want them to be of me?

Now bolster your private cheering section by writing down those things that you do for yourself that provide you with sources of self-confirmation. List all the undeniable achievements that you attained in the past week. They don't have to be major—just positive. List all the things you do well.

Tuck these lists away for that bad day when things go wrong from dawn to dark. On days of seeming (but you can bet they're temporary) failure, review your lists as a reminder that one setback does not a lifetime of disaster make.

Whatever your dreams, it's important to define your vision and use it as a guide to everyday action. You can build an optimal lifestyle in which your work, play, interpersonal relationships, and physical environment are all in harmony with your inner goals and values. Taking risks to facilitate the creation of this special harmony can happen only when you are actively self-supporting, as well as eliciting what you need from others.

Not only is there strength and power in numbers, but women today are finding an exciting new connectedness with each other. You can develop your connectedness through more and better support systems when you feel free to open up and express your feelings. You know there is an element of risk involved in being vulnerable but you reach out anyway. There really is no other way.

Sometimes you may feel trapped in a relationship that is no longer supportive. Perhaps you have outgrown your mentor; perhaps your friend or lover hinders your growth by mocking you, carping at you, or by not being truly glad that you are successfully risking.

When you cannot escape the feeling that it is time to move on, arguments or hurt feelings aside, you must take the big risk of terminating unfulfilling relationships. Refuse to think of this as failure; think of it as reassessment and moving from one plateau to another. Learning to say goodbye is as important as learning to say hello. Remind yourself that life and relationships are temporary and what is really alive and important is what is happening right now.

Summary

Risking can make us feel alone and lonely; yet there are many kinds and sources of support—from close personal relationships to loving pets. Networking is a growing phenomenon more women are choosing, and sometimes a mentor can make all the difference. In the last analysis, however, you are always your own best friend and source of support.

EIGHT

DO IT NOW!

THIS is about to be your finest hour. You have decided your life has a degree of dissatisfaction and you are going to change that. You have done your thinking and preliminary planning and now you're ready to "Go for the Gold."

What's next? Next comes a sweeping away of old fears and uncertainties, making a commitment to yourself, signing a contract with yourself, and making your final action plan.

Saying Goodbye to the Last of the Doubts

If you have postponed making decisions or taking actions in the past, then you will probably reencounter some old, unresolved risks. If you have never allowed yourself to get close to anyone but now you want to get romantically involved, if you have played it safe with civil service types of positions and now you want to start a business for yourself, all the old fears about getting close to another person or your need for job security will be resurrected.

The theme dancing in your head is probably, "Can I really do it? Am I good enough? Brave enough?" In order to make a good decision and commit yourself to action, you must understand why you fear making it and the psychology of losing.

Alfred Adler says he doesn't believe that mental disturbances are illnesses but mistaken lifestyles that perpetuate
feelings of inferiority. For example, neurotics should be considered failures at living, not sick people. They are afraid to
face reality because they cannot accept their inadequacies or
assume responsibility for their action. This may be a harsh
judgment, but Adler goes on to say that people can take action and adjust to any change if it takes place slowly enough,
without making unreasonable demands on the person involved. The bigger and more rapid the change, the greater
the demand involved.

So if you aren't ready for a big change, make a small one.
What's important is that you commit yourself to some action
and do it, even if the step is tiny. Next in importance is for
you to be willing to view any setback not as a failure but as
trial and error.

You are at the critical choice point. Are you going to
sweep out the negative thoughts that have been holding you
back or are you going to let them continue to hold you back
in paralyzing inertia? It's up to you.

Honoring Your Commitment to You

Any real action has to be preceded by commitment. It may
be difficult at first, but the way to go forward is to grit your
teeth and say, "I will!" and mean it and do it. It's easy to walk
up the ladder and out on the high diving board; but committing yourself to jumping off is another matter. With commitment, cold feet and second thoughts won't have a chance.
Without commitment, you may or may not follow through.

Ask yourself this: "Out of all the many things I could do,
which am I willing to commit to? And as a part of my commitment, am I giving myself enough time and resources to
carry out my plan?"

Risk-takers must make a pledge to themselves that they will follow through. The only condition for backing out would be some dramatic new information of which you were unaware when you were doing your planning. You must pledge allegiance to yourself, your goal, and your plan.

Signing a Contract with Yourself

It's time to make an investment in yourself. Excellent ideas are not enough; you must act to create the future you desire and begin to bring it into the present.

Sit down and write out a personal contract. State what you expect to accomplish, in what period of time.

CONTRACT WITH MYSELF

I, _____, will take the following risks:

_____

_____

_____

in order to accomplish the following goal _____

_____

_____.

I will have completed the risks and attained my goal no later than _____.

(date)

Signed_____

Date_____

Make this a binding contract by rewriting it to suit your situation. For instance, you might have more than one goal and there are probably some intermediary steps you need to take.

CONTRACT WITH MYSELF

I, _____ am pledging that

I will make progress toward my goals and in committing to

the following risks:

Goal I: _____

To be achieved by _____
                                         (date)

Risk one: _____

   Work needed to prepare: _____

_____

Risk two: _____

   Work needed to prepare _____

_____

Goal II: _____

To be achieved by _____
                                         (date)

Risk one: _____

Work needed to prepare   _____

_____

Risk two: _____

Work needed to prepare   _____

_____

Update your contract regularly. Remind yourself of your commitment and its timetable. Check off accomplishments and make progress reports to yourself. Once you get started on this process, your sense of achievement will be boundless and will move you forward to the next risk and the next goal.

Make a Specific Action Plan

If you followed the second contract form, you indicated what needed to be done before you were ready to make the risk. This was the beginning of an action plan, perhaps the most important part of the risk-taking process.

Successful people engage in conscious and deliberate planning for change. They shape their lives rather than allow their lives to be shaped by external forces and circumstances. Without planned change we are buffeted and bumped about, the reactors to life rather than the actors in it.

There is little need for planning in a static life where changes are relatively insignificant. Decisions are routine, not exciting; custom and habit play major roles. The active life, however, responds to orderly development and the process of defining purposes and choosing means to obtain your goals. The active life depends upon rational decisions about future goals and takes into account the consequences of alternate courses of action.

Planning involves the setting of objectives, the look at alternatives, a sense of the future and the way things could and ought to be, and action steps. Planning not only achieves results different from those that happenstance brings about, but also anticipates problems sufficiently in advance so that they can be more effectively dealt with. Planning also means that resources will be more efficiently coordinated and used.

The planning process involves the following steps:

1. *What do you have now and what's going on?*

Take inventory and collect data. What's the present situation? What are your strengths and resources to meet the risk ahead? What do you have going for you, physically, socially, intellectually, and spiritually? Does your lifestyle offer you strength? List what you've already tried and the outcomes. (Remember that so-called failures are merely accumulated data.) Check your attitudes. The way you think determines at least 50 percent of the end results. Are your attitudes positive and healthy?

2. *What do you expect to have?*

What is going on in the environment or the context of your risk-taking that will affect the outcome? Make forecasts and projections of trends. If you have your eye on a career change, what are experts saying about the future of the new profession you are contemplating? Is the field on the move and the upswing or on the down and out? Are the signs favorable for what you have in mind? This is where you must be completely honest with yourself. Don't overlook important information because it isn't favorable to your goal.

3. *What do you want?*

The difference between what you have and what you have to have encompasses your goals and objectives. Think of your *goal* as that accomplishment you most want to achieve. Examples: Prepare myself for a better job. Become president of a volunteer agency's board of directors. Think of your *objectives* as the steps necessary to reach your goal, and the timetable necessary to get the whole job done. Here are some examples:

Goal: Prepare myself for a better job by _____
(date)

Objectives: Go back to school and finish the degree (within two years).

Talk to my boss, several of my peers, and as many professionals as possible about career opportunities and what preparation is necessary. (Within six months.)

Get career and aptitude counseling to make sure I'm headed in the best direction for me and for the kinds of fields that are going to have the most openings in the future. (Within two months.)

Join a network of women in my field for support and to make contacts and get referrals. (Within one month.)

Goal: Become president of a volunteer agency's board of directors by _____
(date)

Objectives: Increase volunteer time with the agency for more experience. (Within six months.)

Study agency's program and policies and determine the skills most needed. (Within six months.)

Apply to be appointed to the board of directors. (Within one year.)

Take classes in group communication, leadership, and parliamentary procedure. (Within one year.)

4. *What way is best to get what you want?*

There is always more than one way to reach your goals and objectives. Study alternative courses of action. A successful life is often a matter of making wise choices and compromises. Which is better, on your path to a better job, to go back to school and get more education or increase your work experience, or both? What are the cost and potential reward of each course of action? Lay out as many paths as you can think of and study the prospects and liabilities of each. Go back over your objectives and see if some should be abandoned and new ones added in light of your study of alternatives.

5. *This is the best way to get what you want.*

After you have mentally walked down all the possible paths to your goal, have studied and pondered, it is decision-making time. This looks like the best route for you; you choose it.

Now your action planning has real focus. You have discarded all but the best alternative and can concentrate on details. What approach will you take? What preparation will you have to make? Where can you get help and support? Plan every aspect of what you will say and do. Visualize each step and see yourself succeeding in getting what you want.

6. *Do it!*

Your planning is complete and now it's time for action and implementation. But no, you're not quite through. After you have put your plan in action, you have to take a long look back.

7. *How well did you do and what do you have to do next?*

Evaluation is the final part of the planning process. Through weighing the best and worst of the outcomes, you can learn how to improve the process next time, as well as set the stage for your next cycle of risking and action planning.

Let's work through some specific action plans. These are merely samples and suggestions, of course, and are not meant to be followed exactly. Use them for idea fodder and write out your own.

OVERALL PURPOSE: To raise more money for a better standard of living.

1. *What do you have now and what's going on?*

Because of inflation and some unexpected expenses, you find yourself slipping behind economically. You are barely making it and your savings are being eaten away.

2. *What do you expect to have?*

You don't expect to become a millionaire (at least right away) but you need to do something to make you feel more secure. Apparently inflation is not going to go away and you haven't heard from your fairy godmother lately so something must be done. Your job is interesting, but it doesn't pay very well. It's obvious that the burden is on you to figure out a way to get more money.

3. *What do you want?*

Goal: Increase my income as much as possible.

4. *What way is best to get what you want?*

Alternative no. 1: Ask for a raise from the boss.

Alternative no. 2: Find a second job.

Alternative no. 3: Cut back on expenses and make do with less.

Alternative no. 4: Borrow money and put it into investments.

5. *This is the best way to get what you want.*

After analyzing all four alternatives (and discarding a possible fifth of trying to find a rich man to improve your standard of living) you decide that number one is the most practical. Now you need an action plan to accomplish your chosen alternative.

Goal: Ask the boss for a raise by _____
                                                    (date)

Objective #1: Study best timing to approach the boss.

(Within one month.) Possible steps:

a: Watch boss's mood swings. When is he at his best?

b: Study your own moods. When are you most alert and at your best?

c: What recent project or accomplishment can you point to with pride? What completed work can you use as leverage along with your raise request? How will you answer the boss's question of why you deserve a raise?

Objective #2: Study best place to approach the boss. (Within two weeks.) Possible steps:

a: Is there some way you can get him to come to your office, where you are most comfortable?

b: Is there a neutral place that will work, such as the cafeteria or the conference room?

Objective #3: Decide on dollar range between what you'd like to have and what you'd settle for. (Within two months.) Possible steps:

a: Look up salaries of everyone on your level and with comparable education and experience.

b: Look up salaries of people at your level in other organizations. Find out the true market value of your position. Classified ads, professional societies, and the public library are good places to start.

c: Find out what percentage raise is usually given and for what reasons.

d: Figure out an approach that will encourage the boss to set an amount, rather than you doing it. (If you name a figure, that could become the upper limit in negotiating. What's more, if you have done a good job of explaining why you deserve a raise at this time, the boss's figure may be higher than what you would have asked for.)

Objective #4: Plan a strategy to handle any objections raised by the boss. (Within one month.) Possible steps:

a: Collect as much information as you can about the company's financial condition and, especially, any proof that your department is functioning efficiently and at a profit. Use this to counteract any claim that times are tough and the company can't afford to raise you right now. (Caution: Don't argue on this point. Emphasize your track record and the company's policy of rewarding people who perform well. Stress any good news that you have but don't, in effect, call the boss a liar if he sings the blues about finances.)

b: Plan how you would handle an angry outburst from the boss. When people get hostile toward us, it's tempting to get hostile back, but don't. Mentally rehearse how you will keep your cool and let him get anger or guilt or whatever it is off his chest. Plan how you will listen carefully (even if you are being unfairly dumped on) and try to pick up clues you can use. Plan how you will make sure that your performance is not the cause of the temper tantrum and, if possible, get the boss to say it has nothing to do with you. Draw him out and sympathize with his problems. Remember that many bosses find it very difficult to give out raises and your sitting quietly through a tirade to eventually get what you want is not too high a price to pay.

c: Plan how you would handle the boss's agreeing with you that you deserve a raise but for some mysterious reason he can't give it to you now. Your previous relationship with him will tell you if this is real or phony and, therefore, your best next move.

d: Talk to people who have successfully negotiated raises with your boss or someone like him. Find out what techniques or strategies they used. Some bosses have a regular ritual you are expected to follow. First talk about football scores, then talk about raises.

6. Do it!

You've done your homework, you've prepared your case. You've selected the best time and place and you are ready with answers to any possible objections. So now go do it.

7. *How well did you do and what do you have to do next?*

What happened? Did you get what you wanted, at least in part? Did you get more than you expected? As soon as possible after your encounter, sit down and make notes of everything you can recall of what each of you said and did. Review your notes for clues on what you handled well and what you could improve upon next time. Your 20/20 hindsight is your best asset now in evaluating what happened and also in your future planning.

What you have to do next is start planning for the next round. If you were successful, the next round may not come for six months or a year. If you were not successful (or as successful as you had hoped you'd be) the next round ought to come fairly soon, in about sixty or ninety days. That will give you just time enough to review your action plan and improve it, based on your now being wiser and more experienced in the whole process.

So now you see how to make and follow action plans. No detail is too small to consider because details can often trip us up.

The more thorough your planning, the better chance you will have of taking successful risks and reaching your goals and objectives.

Why Planning Can Fail

All those best-laid plans sometimes don't make it. Here are some pitfalls for you to avoid to make certain that your plans do make it.

1. *Don't do your planning in a vacuum.* Other people are involved in and affected by your potential risk-taking so you

must consider them in your plan. There is also an environment and a context within which your plan will have to work. Do your best to minimize or counteract those conditions outside you to avoid being stymied by circumstances beyond your control.

If you are considering starting your own mail-order business, you would undoubtedly be encouraged by the fact that this is a multibillion-dollar industry. But to face facts, you should also recognize there have been many rags to riches and back to rags stories in what can be a high-risk business. Your planning should encompass the study of both success stories and disasters, and the key factors in each.

2. *Understand the whole process of planning and the significance of each phase.* Some people are planners and some are wingers. But even planners sometimes get impatient and want to skip over some of the aspects and wing it from there.

In your mail-order business example, you might be tempted to do only part of step one, taking inventory and collecting data. You might not have investigated thoroughly enough the specific market for your specific product. Similar products may have been successfully marketed by mail, but what if you have to contend with customer resistance? Perhaps your research ignored the fact that people are basically skeptical and your direct sales letters might be classified as junk mail.

3. *Take plenty of time to plan and implement the plan.* Don't attempt too much at once. It's best to overestimate how long you think each phase of the planning process will take. Don't expect immediate results or *any* results before the entire plan is carried out.

Although you may have worked out a complex plan for your mail-order business, you can avoid unforeseen glitches by starting small and going one step at a time. You could test the market by starting with only one or two products, produced and packaged in your basement in your spare time. Thus, a small financial investment, which you are able and willing to lose if things don't work out, can prevent a later major loss because of planning error.

4. *Understand the difference between planning and doing.* Some people with logical, methodical minds enjoy putting a plan together but they are not capable of carrying it out. Maybe this is why there are think tanks in which bright people generate creative ideas, and administrators who can separate the wild ideas from those that will work. A well-thought-out plan is a thing of beauty. But unless the plan is based in reality and the planner is committed to carrying it out, the beauty is ephemeral, illusive, and virtually useless.

Mail-order businesses exist in the real world and not on paper. There are certain satisfactions in dreaming up possibilities but there is far more payoff when the plan is implemented and not a piece of paper gathering dust on a closet shelf.

5. *Think of your plan as dynamic and fluid, not fixed or static.* Planning is a continuous process and you must be willing to make changes as you go. Plans have to be kept up-to-date and in touch with reality.

Let's say you're just about to launch your mail-order empire when you find out that there are several federal regulations and state trade rules which would affect the way you operate. For example, the Federal Trade Commission has a rule stipulating that goods must be delivered to customers within thirty days, or the customer has the right to cancel. If your plan does not allow for enough staff to keep the filling of orders current, you could be in big trouble. Better revise your plan than get in the middle of lost orders or legal brouhahas.

6. *Your plan has to take the future into account.* Your research will of necessity focus on what has happened before, including case histories of similar products. But your plan

will fail if it doesn't look ahead as well as back. What happened before may not happen again.

The mail-order business has flourished because of the rising cost of gasoline and because people can shop without hassle in their own homes. But what's ahead? What effect will the increasing availability of sophisticated electronic systems have on your projected business? Will you be able to tap into schemes that enable customers to view merchandise and order it via their TV screens? What about rising postal costs? Can your pricing keep up and still give you a profit?

Summary

Your finest hour comes when you are about to take the plunge. You say goodbye to the last of your doubts, you make a commitment to yourself to follow through, and you sign a contract with yourself. Successful risk-taking results when you have worked out a careful and specific action plan, followed each of the seven steps to reach your goals and objectives. Even the best of plans can fail, however, if certain pitfalls are not avoided.

NINE

THE MORNING AFTER

IN THE aftermath of your risk-taking, you need to examine what you did and why and decide if it was worth it. No one but you can fully evaluate what went on and what you got out of it. Only you can weigh the outcomes against your needs and best interests.

In the television movie *See How She Runs*, actress Joanne Woodward played the part of a woman whose goal was to run in the Boston Marathon. There was nothing of consequence going on in her life. She was divorced, a teacher, and the mother of two self-centered teen-age daughters. Life had little excitement.

Her first venture into jogging lasted about two blocks and found her taking a taxi home. But she kept at it, gaining strength and determination gradually, despite being overweight and out of condition, despite being laughed at, rained and snowed on, and being accosted by a would-be rapist.

When that April day dawned in Boston, there she was prancing at the starting gate like the other runners, awaiting the starting gun. She was off and running, feeling confident and knowing that she was making the run just for herself. If she could run twenty-six miles, then she could meet any challenge life had to offer.

Crossing the finish line five-and-a-half hours later, and almost dropping from exhaustion, she knew she had taken a risk and had won. She had proven many things to herself; she had gained insight and motivation. Was it worth it? Decidedly YES!

The completion of any risk in our respective lives signals a time of assessment. Was it really worth it? Would you do it again? What kind of price did you pay? What happened to your self-esteem in the process? Was it elevated or diminished? What changes would you make in future risks of a similar nature? What specific lessons did you learn from this experience?

On the morning after your risk, after you have crossed your emotional finish line, what do you do now? First, *enjoy*. Revel in the exuberance and sense of accomplishment that you have a right to feel. Mentally go over the experiences that led you to this point. You had the guts and determination to see you through.

Traumas of Transition Are Doors to the Future

Society teaches us to avoid or protect ourselves from such transitions in life as divorce, lost jobs, the death of a loved one, relocating, or ending a close relationship. Custom allows us to withdraw and to mourn but doesn't prepare us for the possibilities of rebirth and new beginnings. One door may close, but there are other doors waiting to be opened.

When faced with a trauma of transition, you need first to understand what happened and what the transition stage is. Quick action is not wise; live through the experience and consider options before grabbing at what might turn out to be an unwise choice of action. Next become aware of who you are in relation to the transition. Try to cope positively with the trauma by taking advantage of the affirmative growth possibilities offered by even the most emotionally wrenching transition.

It is your choice whether you stay in trauma longer than necessary or whether you risk an exciting rebirth. Living in the past, mourning your loss, and avoiding new growth may be natural for a while. But continue them too long and you are committing emotional suicide.

Detaching ourselves from our former selves is a form of dying, too. You feel a vague sense of nostalgia, as though something of yourself is being left behind, which it is. The old, unproductive, inhibiting thoughts and behavior are being left behind so that you can have a rebirth of awareness to chart your course on a more meaningful life.

Handling the Inevitable Letdown
After It's Over

Judy Garland used to receive standing ovations after risking spilling her emotions out in song. Audiences loved her for sharing herself. They applauded, whistled, and stood long after the curtain had dropped to let her know they appreciated her and her efforts. Although she would leave the stage buoyed by the response, a few hours later she would sit in her hotel suite in an acute stage of depression.

This letdown is predictable and normal. A well-known writer, who has published seven books, confides that each time she completes a writing project she feels a great sense of loss. She hates having to say goodbye to an effort that took a major part of her attention and energy for a considerable period of time. She usually has to spend at least six weeks recovering from the letdown after a book is completed.

Emma emerged from the courtroom. It was finally over. After three years of litigation over a sex discrimination suit against her former employer, she had won. Yet somehow she couldn't rejoice over her victory. She was still too close to memories of the rejection she had experienced from other women at the factory. Although many of them had similar grievances, they were afraid to risk their jobs to take legal action. Instead of admiring Emma's courage and viewing her as a champion of their mutual cause, they viewed her with suspicion and distrust. They shunned her.

Emma risked the suit and while it was ever so slowly progressing through the courts, she experienced one loss after another. First she lost her job and had to go on welfare. No one would hire her because the suit labeled her as a first-class troublemaker.

She finally got a job in a temporary employment agency but she wasn't making enough money to take care of herself and her two children. She decided to take still another risk and start her own business. Since she had always been good with tools and liked doing handyman chores around the house, she began doing chores for others. She advertised her availability, stressing that she specialized in helping working women. Soon the business was going well, so she decided to add house painting.

So now here she was, with a successful business plus $50,000 from the court settlement and instead of feeling happy, she felt let down.

Postpartum blues is a term familiar to any woman who has given birth. Within two weeks after the birth of a child, many women experience a sense of depression. Psychologists say this is due to the long waiting, as well as the awe and dread of the mysterious unknown.

Any change in status creates new adjustments. Whether giving birth to a new idea, career, relationship, or child, a transition time is inevitable and necessary. Accepting and recognizing that you will have times of emptiness, moodiness, mild depression, and even feel a bit off balance emotionally, are required as you risk venturing into the unknown.

Fortunately, this stage is temporary. There need not be any fear of prolonged emotional upheaval. Remembering that this, too, will pass, can help you get through the difficult time of letdown.

Women who are seasoned risk-takers have a variety of ways of dealing with this aspect of risking. One woman finds the saddest movie or television drama she can, and works her way through a box of tissues, sobbing out her frustrations. Another woman reports that she bangs on her piano to work out the letdown feeling. She says it may take as long as two weeks and piles of musical scores before she is ready to resume living. Some people tap-dance or jog or play racketball or dig in the garden to offset the letdown feeling.

Many people report that during the time of transition after a risk is over they experience a sense of isolation and need to be by themselves. This is a necessary time of assessment, the emptying out or the dying before new life can begin. Although it may not be a happy time, it is tolerable and it signals that new growth and awareness, as well as the appetite for new risk-taking, are on their way.

Keeping Your Eye on the Next Risk and Not the Last

Off in the distance you see the new dawn. You somehow got through the transitions and traumas and find yourself ready to risk again. The curtain has fallen on yesterday's risking drama. What will give your life new meaning and pizzazz today? What new situation will arise to test your competence, abilities, and courage?

Assuming that you have done your best with the past risk,

you can borrow momentum from it for trying the next one. Let's say your most recent risk was to break out of middle management and strike out for the top of the organizational heap. You won. There you are in your new corner office. What will be your next risk? Daring to change policies from traditionally conservative to something more imaginative? Or reorganizing the system? If you have been successful in your last venture, you can plan better, your goals become more clear, and you can act without the hesitation that might have accompanied your previous risk.

Keep your eye on the new target, however. Don't dwell on or keep reliving the past no matter how triumphant. The secret for risking the morning after is to perpetuate your yearning for a better life for yourself, to be better off than you are. This doesn't mean that you have to have an insatiable urge to own all the goodies of life. It means, instead, that you are able to set your sights on attainable goals, and are willing to invest 100 percent of your energy and ability behind the risk.

It means that you plan to climb the mountain one step at a time, without looking back or down. It means you are present- and future-oriented and that your next risk will reflect not only your present goal but also your vision of what might be.

Seeing the Advantages in Losing As Well as Winning

Even if you reached only part of your goal, that too is accomplishment. Or if you didn't reach it at all, you have still gathered a lot of data that will improve your performance for the next big gamble. As you know, you learn far more from your mistakes than from your triumphs.

If it didn't turn out as you expected or your goal exceeded

your grasp, don't be too discouraged or despairing. If you look at losing objectively, you can see a number of ways you can profit and also turn what looks like a failure into a success.

If egos are so frail that they cannot admit even the slightest mistake or defeat, they are bound some day to see their small mistakes turned into large ones. For every heroine who goes ahead to overcome what looks like insurmountable odds, there are hundreds of people who compound their losses, dwelling on them, and allowing small defeats to be viewed as disasters.

Strength is tempered by adversity. The Orientals have a saying, "The rice grain suffers under the blow of the pestle, but admire its whiteness once the ordeal is over." Too many of us approach life convinced that victory is thrilling but defeat is agony. Seldom are we faced with those extremes. Even the greatest victory may have a catch to it and even the most devastating defeat usually has elements of success. At least you tried. And that's better than not trying. At least you know what not to do next time. And that is more educational than having victories come your way too easily to be appreciated. You profit from a loss by having the courage to face it, learn from it, then put it behind you.

Many women have been conditioned to feel stupid when they make mistakes, to expect humiliation when their errors or failures come to light. Such attitudes are hard to shake. But admitting mistakes can be a source of growth. If you have only known successes, your perspective of the world and your self-concept will be distorted. With no balancing setbacks in your experience, you could easily exaggerate your abilities and underestimate the risks in future endeavors. Your overconfidence could interfere with sound judgment and sooner or later you would be sure to have a royal flop.

For a woman who has no previous experience with failure, losing could be a shattering ordeal rather than an experience to be viewed philosophically. But losing in itself has no merit. What you do as a result of the defeat is significant. Losing can either destroy you or make you stronger. Which will it be?

Either success or failure can raise questions: did you do your best; did you plan carefully enough; and did you grow in character and depth? Without loss, many great discoveries of life would have been missed. When an inventor was asked why he wasn't discouraged after more than two hundred attempts to perfect his invention had failed, he replied, "Because now I know more than two hundred ways that won't work."

Yesterday's You in Today's Mirror
Looking Toward Tomorrow

Risking offers new self-discoveries that enable more and better risking to occur. For some women, the more that is accomplished, the more old fears reappear. Sometimes it's more comfortable to hide behind a role or assume a pseudo-sophisticated air of "I don't care."

If, however, you have put everything behind your risk and kept forging ahead despite old fears, you can reach a point where you take your losses and successes with equal honesty and equanimity. Facing that moment of truth is the apex of the morning after.

You are in the process of creating a better life for yourself by accepting and welcoming your destiny, giving up pretenses and attempting to become what you suspect you could be if you pushed a little harder. The final thrust is a solitary act where you step out in space or on to a new frontier. No one can know or comprehend what you are becoming except yourself.

You have learned to appreciate and trust yourself. Johnson and Ferguson put it this way: "Trusting ourselves means believing in our own perceptions, our own expertise, and our own values as women—even if others see it differently."*

At this time, there is no shared glory. Your vision of your new world is yours alone. You created it. People who care about you will feel joy in your triumph and those who feel threatened or jealous of your achievement will find reasons why your accomplishment really wasn't all that great.

But you know your efforts have worth and that's what counts. You made your life a creative work of art. Out of confusion and uncertainty, you grew into a special and unique person. You have drawn from your own inner strength to realize your goal. Perhaps you walked through fire but as Nietzsche said, "One must still have chaos to give birth to a dancing star."

You have followed your inner dream. You have learned how to take risks with your head high and your eyes bright. You are woman. You are invincible. You have won.

Summary

The morning after taking a risk is the time to evaluate and decide if it was worth it. It usually is, even if you lost, because there are advantages in losing as well as winning. Transition periods may be traumatic but they also provide doors to future opportunities and new beginnings. Don't be discouraged if, after it's all over, you feel let down instead of triumphant. That's natural. As you move from risk to risk, keep your eye on the target ahead. Be sure to take today's risk and not yesterday's.

*Karen Johnson, M.D., and Tom Ferguson, *Trusting Ourselves: The Complete Guide To Emotional Well-Being For Women*. (New York: The Atlantic Monthly Press, 1990), p. 464.

For more information about risk-taking or related subjects,
write to the authors:

Betsy Morscher, Ph.D.
Betsy Morscher & Associates
787 Elizabeth St., Denver, Colorado 80218
303-322-5522

Barbara Schindler Jones, Ph.D.
Communication Consultant
6442 Glenmoor Rd., Boulder, Colorado 80303
303-499-5622